THE FOLGER LIBRARY SHAKESPEARE

Designed to make Shakespeare's classic plays available to the general reader, each edition contains a reliable text with modernized spelling and punctuation, scene-by-scene plot summaries, and explanatory notes clarifying obscure and obsolete expressions. An interpretive essay and accounts of Shakespeare's life and theater form an instructive preface to each play.

Louis B. Wright, General Editor, was the Director of the Folger Shakespeare Library from 1948 until his retirement in 1968. He is the author of *Middle-Class Culture in Elizabethan England, Religion and Empire, Shakespeare for Everyman,* and many other books and essays on the history and literature of the Tudor and Stuart periods.

Virginia Lamar, Assistant Editor, served as research assistant to the Director and Executive Secretary of the Folger Shakespeare Library from 1946 until her death in 1968. She is the author of *English Dress in the Age of Shakespeare* and *Travel and Roads in England,* and coeditor of William Strachey's *Historie of Travell into Virginia Britania.*

The Folger Shakespeare Library

The Folger Library General Reader's Shakespeare

THE TRAGEDY OF
RICHARD
THE SECOND

by
WILLIAM
SHAKESPEARE

WASHINGTON SQUARE PRESS
PUBLISHED BY POCKET BOOKS NEW YORK

A Washington Square Press Publication of
POCKET BOOKS, a division of Simon & Schuster, Inc.
1230 Avenue of the Americas, New York, N.Y. 10020

ISBN: 0-671-53142-5

First Pocket Books printing September, 1962

18   17   16   15   14   13   12

WASHINGTON SQUARE PRESS, WSP and colophon are
registered trademarks of Simon & Schuster, Inc.

Printed in the U.S.A.

Preface

This edition of *Richard the Second* is designed to make available a readable text of one of Shakespeare's less familiar plays. In the centuries since Shakespeare many changes have occurred in the meanings of words, and some clarification of Shakespeare's vocabulary may be helpful. To provide the reader with necessary notes in the most accessible format, we have placed them on the pages facing the text that they explain. We have tried to make these notes as brief and simple as possible. Preliminary to the text we have also included a brief statement of essential information about Shakespeare and his stage. Readers desiring more detailed information should refer to the books suggested in the references, and if still further information is needed, the bibliographies in those books will provide the necessary clues to the literature of the subject.

The early texts of all of Shakespeare's plays provide only inadequate stage directions, and it is conventional for modern editors to add many that clarify the action. Such additions, and additions to entrances, are placed in square brackets.

All illustrations are from material in the Folger Library collections.

L. B. W.

V. A. L.

February 1, 1962

Incompetent King and Fated Usurper

In *Richard II* Shakespeare chose to portray a weak
and arbitrary king who at last is dethroned by a
man strong and daring enough to raise his hand
against God's anointed ruler, an act of profanation
that brings upon his line ultimate disaster in the
third generation. The theme of this play was of
enormous interest to Shakespeare's contemporaries,
for it had political overtones of vital concern to
every Englishman who lived in fear of the chaos
that might ensue if Elizabeth the Queen died without an heir and left the fate of the kingdom to
quarreling favorites. When *Richard II* was first performed, enemies of the Queen were whispering that
she too was surrounded by timeserving advisers like
those who had helped Richard waste away his
patrimony. The Queen herself knew that the paral-
lel between herself and the unfortunate Plantagenet
was being made by some of her subjects. To William Lambarde, the antiquary and legal historian,
she commented on August 4, 1601, "I am Richard
II, know ye not that."

This does not mean that Shakespeare set out

deliberately to write a play on a burning political issue and to meddle in matters of state. It does mean, however, that he picked a topic that quickly came to have meanings that Shakespeare never dreamed of when he sat down to put his play together. As a shrewd dramatist seeking timely topics of concern to the theatregoing public, he knew of course that Richard's life and rule would make a play that would be of interest; otherwise he would not have selected that topic. But he could not foresee that six years after the play was first performed the Earl of Essex would set himself up as another Bolingbroke and rebel against the Queen, or that some of Essex's followers would hire Shakespeare's company of actors to perform a play of the deposing and killing of Richard II, a play acted on February 7, 1601, the afternoon before Essex's rising on February 8. Presumably this play was Shakespeare's own *Richard II*, which the conspirators thought suitable to stir the fainthearted among them to rebellion. Shakespeare's company was later called to account for this unwitting participation in the plot and exonerated; Shakespeare himself was not censured. Obviously the authorities did not consider his play a deliberate contribution to subversion. The conspirators had merely confirmed Shakespeare's hunch that the theme was of startling public interest.

Shakespeare's *Richard II* was written for the Lord Chamberlain's Men, Shakespeare's own company, and appears to have been first performed in the season of 1595–1596. A quarto version was first printed in 1597 and the popularity of the play was such that two quarto versions appeared in 1598, a fourth quarto in 1608, a fifth quarto in 1615, and a sixth quarto in 1634, after the printing in the First Folio of 1623. It is significant that the deposition scene was omitted in the first three quartos and not inserted until the fourth quarto of 1608 when James I had been on the throne for five years. Even so, the title page of this quarto bearing the words, "With some new additions of the Parliament scene, and the deposing of King Richard, as it hath been lately acted by the King's Majesty's servants at the Globe," was canceled in some copies and the offending wording about the deposition left out. In the course of production either the printer got worried about calling attention to this sensational scene or the authorities ordered the title page changed. The fifth quarto of 1615 finally restored to the title page the wording about the deposition. Although King James himself had about his throne some unsavory favorites who might have matched evil reputations with any who misled Richard II, evidently such parallels were no longer believed to be politically dangerous.

Critics have expended much ink in discussing Shakespeare's purpose in *Richard II* and his interpretation of both Richard and Bolingbroke. To one he makes Richard more a poet than a king; to another Richard is primarily an actor carried away with a morbid fascination in the part that he has to play. To some readers, Richard is the personification of weakness and effeminacy; other readers see in Shakespeare's treatment a desire to win sympathy for a king who lacked the stern qualities needed for his role but who was a gentle and artistic soul. William Butler Yeats, for example, thinks that Shakespeare's sympathies were with Richard, the dreamy poet, and that he could not possibly have had any fellow feeling for the cold, hard, calculating Bolingbroke who dethroned this contemplative artist. Sir Edmund Chambers, on the other hand, in refuting this notion, declares that Shakespeare was not a Celtic idealist but "an honest burgess of Saxon Stratford" who had a thorough appreciation of Bolingbroke's practical qualities and could contrast the two natures with complete objectivity. What the modern reader is likely to forget is that Shakespeare was studying a type of kingship from a strictly Tudor point of view.

Another point to remember is that Shakespeare was still writing under the influence of Christopher Marlowe, whose technique had been to concentrate action and interest upon the study of a single individual, as in *Tamburlaine, Doctor Faustus,* and *The Jew of Malta.* Marlowe had also written in *Edward II* a play on a king whose circumstances somewhat paralleled those of Richard II. Furthermore, in Marlowe Shakespeare had an example of lyrical extravagance that is manifest in the speeches of Richard. The last play Shakespeare had written before *Richard II* was *Romeo and Juliet,* and Shakespeare was still writing in the lyrical mood of that play. *Richard II* shows evidence of hasty composition and contains many lines that Shakespeare could have revised to his profit, but into the mouth of Richard he puts singing verse that lives in the memory.

Shakespeare was profoundly interested in the history of England as a source for drama, but he did not set to work like a historian to present the story of England's past in chronological sequence. His first history play was perhaps the second part of *Henry VI*, and from then on he patched about in the chronology as his own interest or the needs of his company dictated. *Richard III*, a play on the reign that ended the Wars of the Roses, came before *Richard II*, which dramatized the episodes beginning that long and bloody conflict. No one knows what prompted Shakespeare's sequence of composition, but once all the history plays were completed he had consecutive dramas that illuminated the background of the Tudor age and presented a fairly coherent political doctrine, particularly in its revelation of the theory of kingship.

Richard II is the first of four plays dealing with the incompetent reign of Richard, the usurpation of Henry Bolingbroke and the establishment of his rule, and the glories of victory over the French in the reign of the hero-king, Henry V. Whether Shakespeare had in mind a tetralogy when he wrote *Richard II*, one will never know. But he clearly was fascinated by the problems and theories of kingship, and he may have decided while working on *Richard II* to continue the dramatic study with the working out of destiny in *Henry IV, Parts 1* and *2*, and *Henry V*. In the meantime, he interrupted the series to write *The Merchant of Venice, King John,* and, perhaps, *Much Ado About Nothing.*

Richard was the son of Edward Prince of Wales, known since Elizabethan times as Edward the Black Prince. The Black Prince, the son and heir of Edward III, died before his father, and young Richard succeeded to the throne in 1377 at the age of ten. His uncle, John of Gaunt, had received from Edward III palatine powers for his great Duchy of Lancaster, which made Gaunt for all practical purposes the ruler of more than half of England, for the King's writ did not run in his palatinate. Another uncle, Thomas of Woodstock, Duke of Gloucester, had dared to threaten at one point to remove Richard from the throne, and at last was arrested for treason and confined to Calais Castle, where in the autumn of 1397 he was murdered. Throughout the play the dead Duke is referred to as "noble Gloucester," though historically he was bellicose and self-seeking. A third uncle, Edmund of Langley, Duke of York, who served as Regent when Richard went on the second expedition to Ireland, had little competence and is characterized by Shakespeare as almost a comic character.

The historical time span covered by *Richard II* is from April 29, 1398, until March 12, 1400, the last of Richard's reign. The play opens at Windsor Castle with a hearing of a dispute between Henry Bolingbroke, Duke of Hereford, the son of John of Gaunt, and Thomas Mowbray, Duke of Norfolk. This hearing was the culmination of a long cycle of events, which began in 1387 with a struggle for power led by the Duke of Gloucester and a faction known as the Five Appellants, of which Boling-broke was one. They managed to browbeat and circumvent Richard, and for a time to replace his favorites at court with their own adherents. The latest biographer of Richard, Harold F. Hutchison, in *The Hollow Crown,* thinks that Richard's de-termination to wreak revenge upon the Five Appel-lants and his other enemies and to free himself from their domination explains his actions during the remainder of the reign. Bolingbroke and Mowbray had both been members of Gloucester's faction, the Five Appellants of 1387, and they alone had es-caped disgrace or death. As yet Richard had held his hand against these two, perhaps because Mow-bray had turned witness against his colleagues, and because Bolingbroke was old John of Gaunt's son and Richard was not ready to alienate Gaunt by disgracing his son.

But now the sometime colleagues against the King had quarreled. Bolingbroke charged that Mowbray, a month before the session of Parliament at Shrewsbury in 1398, had reminded him that Richard bore them both an enmity and that they should take action before it was too late. Boling-broke revealed this to Richard just before the meeting of Parliament and claimed that he had indignantly refused to have anything to do with a treasonable suggestion. Bolingbroke was doubtless bitter against Mowbray because he had turned Crown's evidence against his uncle Gloucester and had been captain of Calais when Gloucester was

murdered there. Mowbray in turn charged Bolingbroke with treason. This famous quarrel placed
both of Richard's enemies on the defensive and
was the background of the opening scene in the
play.

Shakespeare in *Richard II* concentrates upon a
shorter period of time than is characteristic of most
of his history plays. From the posing of the problem
raised by the Bolingbroke-Mowbray dispute until
the denouement, the time covered is about eighteen
months. The action moves swiftly with no distrac-
tions of subplot such as *Henry IV* contained.

In the beginning, Richard has the initiative, with
the opportunity of destroying his enemies and es-
tablishing firmly the royal authority. As Shakespeare
works out the details of the plot, Richard throws
away his advantage by listening to the advice of
frivolous favorites, by ill-considered actions and injustice, by disregarding the good of the realm, by
his greed in appropriating the lands and possessions
of John of Gaunt, and by his vacillating weakness
in moments of crisis. As Shakespeare portrays him,
Richard is precisely the kind of king that no
thoughtful citizen of Tudor England could approve.
Of all situations in the body politic, the one that
Elizabethans deplored most was weakness in the
sovereign that invited rebellion and civil disturb-
ance. The memories of the chaos of the Wars of the
Roses still lingered and the Elizabethans wanted no
return of such anarchy. If Shakespeare found himself entranced by the spectacle of a poetic king in
conflict with harsh realities as Yeats believed, he

never wavered in his Tudor concept of Richard as the opposite of what a king should be. Indeed, that is one of Shakespeare's purposes in writing the play. If he had been carried away with sympathy for Richard he could never have gone on to create in the person of Henry V his ideal of a hero-king.

But the treatment of the problems raised by Richard's incompetence and deposition were not simple for Shakespeare. As Miss Lily Bess Campbell points out in *Shakespeare's "Histories": Mirrors of Elizabethan Policy*, "Shakespeare here set forth a political problem that was engaging the interest of the nation and . . . set it forth fairly. He did not ask whether a good king might be deposed, but whether a king might be deposed for any cause. He used Richard II as the accepted pattern of a deposed king, but he used his pattern to set forth the political ethics of the Tudors in regard to the rights and duties of a king. It might equally well have served as a warning to Elizabeth and to any who desired to usurp her throne. The way of the transgressing king was shown to be hard, but no happiness was promised to the one who tried to execute God's vengeance or to depose the deputy elected by the Lord."

Shakespeare's treatment of history in *Richard II* is completely anachronistic, for Shakespeare is an Elizabethan dramatist, not an antiquarian intent upon re-creating a section of the Middle Ages. Historically, Richard was a medieval king operating in an environment that had not yet discovered nationalism. For Richard and his contemporaries,

England was a feudal patrimony that the king could deal with in accordance with his power and capacity, even to the extent of alienating portions of the territory and awarding it to his friends and kin, as Edward III had done in turning over the Duchy of Lancaster to John of Gaunt as a virtually independent palatinate. Yet Shakespeare reflects the new nationalism that had developed under the Tudors, particularly in the reign of Elizabeth, and he puts into the mouth of John of Gaunt—of all people—perhaps the most patriotic speech in the whole of the Shakespeare canon:

> This royal throne of kings, this scept'red isle,
> This earth of majesty, this seat of Mars,
> This other Eden, demiparadise,
> This fortress built by Nature for herself
> Against infection and the hand of war,
> This happy breed of men, this little world,
> This precious stone set in the silver sea,
> Which serves it in the office of a wall,
> Or as a moat defensive to a house,
> Against the envy of less happier lands;
> This blessed plot, this earth, this realm, this England.

This speech, which is wholly Shakespeare's invention, has been constantly quoted in periods of crisis in England's later history and printed in anthologies as the noblest expression of a patriot, a word and a sentiment that would have been unknown to the historical Gaunt. But it illustrates Shakespeare's own reflection of public feeling toward the realm of England, and it suggests another reason why a play like that of *Richard II* and the sequels building up to *Henry V* had so much appeal for the audiences at the Globe.

STAGE HISTORY

In view of the application that spectators could make to their own times, it is surprising that *Richard II* was permitted at all on the Elizabethan stage. Despite the Queen's recognition that she could be identified with Richard, the play appears to have enjoyed a normal run in Shakespeare's theatre. Not until Essex's conspirators persuaded Augustine Phillips, manager of the Lord Chamberlain's company, to revive what he described as an old play did the portrayal of Richard on the stage become a matter of governmental concern. Essex was accused at his trial of having seen frequent performances of *Richard II*, presumably Shakespeare's play, though in 1611 the company had another play on this subject which may have dated from an earlier time. Queen Elizabeth told Lambarde that a play on the theme of Richard II had been given "forty times in open streets and houses."

During the reign of James, Shakespeare's *Richard II* had a revival, if we can believe the canceled title page of the quarto of 1608, which described the play as "lately acted by the King's Majesty's servants at the Globe." On the accession of James, Shakespeare's company, the Lord Chamberlain's Men, became the King's Men. Sailors on board the ship *Dragon*, commanded by Captain William Keeling, put on a performance of *Richard II* off Sierra

Leone on September 30, 1607. The play had a revival at the Globe in 1631. After the Restoration,
Nahum Tate made an adaptation that ran for two
days in 1680 before it was suppressed by order of
Charles II's authorities. Tate changed the setting
to Italy, but the play was destined to ill success.
Lewis Theobald, a generation later in 1719, made
an adaptation that ran for two seasons. *Richard II*
was revived at Covent Garden in 1738 but it was
not one of the plays that excited the eighteenth
century. From time to time in the nineteenth century it had revivals. Charles Kean in 1857 staged an
elaborately adapted version with much pageantry,
which had a run of eighty-five days. In the twen-
tieth century, many of the great Elizabethan actors
have performed in *Richard II.* Margaret Webster
directed a revival in New York in 1937 with Maurice
Evans as Richard, which was so popular that it ran
for 171 performances. In 1961, in the television
performance of Shakespeare's history plays entitled
"An Age of Kings," *Richard II* was one of the most
effective plays, perhaps because of the excellent
rendering of Richard's poetic lines.

SOURCES

Scholars have long argued about the sources for
Richard II and agreement has been less than unani-
mous. The main and obvious source is Raphael
Holinshed's *The Chronicles of England, Scotland,
and Ireland* (2nd ed., 1587), which in turn bor-
rowed from Edward Hall's *The Union of the Two*

Noble and Illustrate Families of Lancaster and York (1548). These chronicles present the history of Richard's reign from a Lancastrian point of view and blacken the King's character. Shakespeare took over this traditional and hostile characterization without question. Hutchison in *The Hollow Crown* shows that the historical Richard was a far different person from the one the Lancastrian chronicles portray.

Shakespeare seems to have known and used Samuel Daniel's *The First Four Books of the Civil Wars between the Two Houses of Lancaster and York* (1595). Some scholars, however, have contended that Daniel's poem came out too late for Shakespeare to use and the indebtedness was on the other side.

Shakespeare also shows evidence of an acquaintance with an old play preserved in manuscript without a title page, generally called *Thomas of Woodstock,* which treats the death of the Duke of Gloucester. He may also have read *The Chronicle of Froissart,* translated by Lord Berners (1523–1525). Two French chronicles contemporary with Richard and more favorable to him existed in Shakespeare's time only in manuscript but were known to some of the Elizabethan chroniclers. If Shakespeare made direct use of these French manuscripts, the fact is not obvious in the play. He may have found hints for his treatment of Richard and his references to Gloucester in the popular old metrical collection of tales, *A Mirror for Magistrates* (1559), though the play shows no evidence of borrowing from this source.

Professor John Dover Wilson in his edition of the play contended that Shakespeare used for his source an old play now lost, and that he reworded this play without even reading Holinshed. This is a tempting thesis in the light of Shakespeare's use of old plays elsewhere, but no evidence exists for a prototype play of *Richard II*.

Despite all the suggestions of diverse sources, it is clear that Shakespeare's primary source was Holinshed. From other sources he may have picked up hints for this and that, but he was capable of creating scenes like the deathbed of John of Gaunt, the garden scene, the episode with the mirror in the deposition scene, the representation of the child-bride Isabel as a grown woman, and Henry's lamentation at the end of the play over Richard's murder. It is hard for research scholars to conceive of a Shakespeare not working as they would work—by going to the library and running down every possible detail of the life of his subject. But Shakespeare had no convenient public library with an efficient reference service, and he was frightfully busy just at the time he was writing *Richard II*. He had completed three plays for the season of 1594–1595, and, in addition to *Richard II*, he got ready for the season of 1595–1596 *A Midsummer Night's Dream* and had in preparation *King John* and *The Merchant of Venice* for the season of 1596–1597. It is not reasonable to believe that Shakespeare went searching about for surviving French manuscript chronicles of

Richard's reign, or that he even looked for hard-to-come-by old printed books for additional material if Holinshed seemed sufficient. He had other things on his mind.

THE TEXT

The present text, like most of the modern editions of *Richard II*, is based on the first quarto version of 1597, which may have been printed from the author's manuscript. The later quartos are all derived successively from the preceding. The copy for the First Folio version of this play appears to have been one of the quartos, probably Quarto 5, which had been partially collated with Quarto 1. The deposition scene, first inserted in Quarto 4 (1608), may have been recovered from the memory of some actor or taken down by shorthand. It was probably normally played on the stage from the beginning but omitted in the three first quarto printings. All the early versions of the play have many errors. The present editors have compared the texts of both the early editions and those of previous editors and made the minimum of corrections and emendations that seemed required.

THE AUTHOR

As early as 1598 Shakespeare was so well known as a literary and dramatic craftsman that Francis Meres, in his *Palladis Tamia: Wits Treasury*, referred in flattering terms to him as "mellifluous and honey-tongued Shakespeare," famous for his *Venus and Adonis,* his *Lucrece,* and "his sugared sonnets," which were circulating "among his private friends." Meres observes further that "as Plautus and Seneca are accounted the best for comedy and tragedy among the Latins, so Shakespeare among the English is the most excellent in both kinds for the stage," and he mentions a dozen plays that had made a name for Shakespeare. He concludes with the remark "that the Muses would speak with Shakespeare's fine filed phrase if they would speak English."

To those acquainted with the history of the Elizabethan and Jacobean periods, it is incredible that anyone should be so naïve or ignorant as to doubt the reality of Shakespeare as the author of the plays that bear his name. Yet so much nonsense has been written about other "candidates" for the plays that it is well to remind readers that no credible evidence that would stand up in a court of law has ever been adduced to prove either that Shakespeare did not write his plays or that anyone else wrote them. All the theories offered for the authorship of Francis Bacon, the Earl of Derby, the Earl of Oxford, the Earl of Hertford, Christopher Marlowe, and a score of other candidates are mere conjectures spun from the active imaginations of persons who confuse hypothesis and conjecture with evidence.

As Meres' statement of 1598 indicates, Shakespeare was already a popular playwright whose name carried weight at the box office. The obvious

Shakespear ý Player by Garter

Sketch of Shakespeare's coat of arms.
From a sixteenth-century manuscript.

reputation of Shakespeare as early as 1598 makes the effort to prove him a myth one of the most absurd in the history of human perversity.

The anti-Shakespeareans talk darkly about a plot of vested interests to maintain the authorship of Shakespeare. Nobody has any vested interest in Shakespeare, but every scholar is interested in the truth and in the quality of evidence advanced by special pleaders who set forth hypotheses in place of facts.

The anti-Shakespeareans base their arguments upon a few simple premises, all of them false. These false premises are that Shakespeare was an unlettered yokel without any schooling, that nothing is known about Shakespeare, and that only a noble lord or the equivalent in background could have written the plays. The facts are that more is known about Shakespeare than about most dramatists of his day, that he had a very good education, acquired in the Stratford Grammar School, that the plays show no evidence of profound book learning, and that the knowledge of kings and courts evident in the plays is no greater than any intelligent young man could have picked up at second hand. Most anti-Shakespeareans are naïve and betray an obvious snobbery. The author of their favorite plays, they imply, must have had a college diploma framed and hung on his study wall like the one in their dentist's office, and obviously so great a writer must have had a title or some equally significant evidence of exalted social background. They forget that genius has a way of cropping up in unexpected places and that none of the great creative writers of the world got his inspiration in a college or university course.

William Shakespeare was the son of John Shakespeare of Stratford-upon-Avon, a substantial citizen of that small but busy market town in the center of the rich agricultural county of Warwick. John Shakespeare kept a shop, what we would call a general store; he dealt in wool and other produce and gradually acquired property. As a youth, John Shakespeare had learned the trade of glover and leather worker. There is no contemporary evidence that the elder Shakespeare was a butcher, though the anti-Shakespeareans like to talk about the ignorant "butcher's boy of Stratford." Their only evidence is a statement by gossipy John Aubrey, more than a century after William Shakespeare's birth, that young William followed his father's trade, and when he killed a calf, "he would do it in a high style and make a speech." We would like to believe the story true, but Aubrey is not a very credible witness.

John Shakespeare probably continued to operate a farm at Snitterfield that his father had leased. He married Mary Arden, daughter of his father's landlord, a man of some property. The third of their eight children was William, baptized on April 26, 1564, and probably born three days before. At least, it is conventional to celebrate April 23 as his birthday.

The Stratford records give considerable information about John Shakespeare. We know that he held

several municipal offices including those of alderman and mayor. In 1580 he was in some sort of
legal difficulty and was fined for neglecting a summons of the Court of Queen's Bench requiring him
to appear at Westminster and be bound over to
keep the peace.

As a citizen and alderman of Stratford, John
Shakespeare was entitled to send his son to the
grammar school free. Though the records are lost,
there can be no reason to doubt that this is where
young William received his education. As any student of the period knows, the grammar schools provided the basic education in Latin learning and literature. The Elizabethan grammar school is not to
be confused with modern grammar schools. Many
cultivated men of the day received all their formal
education in the grammar schools. At the universities in this period a student would have received
little training that would have inspired him to be a
creative writer. At Stratford young Shakespeare
would have acquired a familiarity with Latin and
some little knowledge of Greek. He would have
read Latin authors and become acquainted with
the plays of Plautus and Terence. Undoubtedly, in
this period of his life he received that stimulation
to read and explore for himself the world of ancient
and modern history which he later utilized in his
plays. The youngster who does not acquire this
type of intellectual curiosity *before* college days
rarely develops as a result of a college course the
kind of mind Shakespeare demonstrated. His learning in books was anything but profound, but he

clearly had the probing curiosity that sent him in search of information, and he had a keenness in the observation of nature and of humankind that finds reflection in his poetry.

There is little documentation for Shakespeare's boyhood. There is little reason why there should be. Nobody knew that he was going to be a dramatist about whom any scrap of information would be prized in the centuries to come. He was merely an active and vigorous youth of Stratford, perhaps assisting his father in his business, and no Boswell bothered to write down facts about him. The most important record that we have is a marriage license issued by the Bishop of Worcester on November 27, 1582, to permit William Shakespeare to marry Anne Hathaway, seven or eight years his senior; furthermore, the Bishop permitted the marriage after reading the banns only once instead of three times, evidence of the desire for haste. The need was explained on May 26, 1583, when the christening of Susanna, daughter of William and Anne Shakespeare, was recorded at Stratford. Two years later, on February 2, 1585, the records show the birth of twins to the Shakespeares, a boy and a girl who were christened Hamnet and Judith.

What William Shakespeare was doing in Stratford during the early years of his married life, or when he went to London, we do not know. It has been conjectured that he tried his hand at schoolteaching, but that is a mere guess. There is a legend that he left Stratford to escape a charge of poaching in the park of Sir Thomas Lucy of Charle-

cote, but there is no proof of this. There is also a
legend that when first he came to London, he
earned his living by holding horses outside a playhouse and presently was given employment inside,
but there is nothing better than eighteenth-century
hearsay for this. How Shakespeare broke into the
London theatres as a dramatist and actor we do not
know. But lack of information is not surprising, for
Elizabethans did not write their autobiographies,
and we know even less about the lives of many
writers and some men of affairs than we know
about Shakespeare. By 1592 he was so well estab-
lished and popular that he incurred the envy of the
dramatist and pamphleteer Robert Greene, who referred to him as an "upstart crow . . . in his own
conceit the only Shake-scene in a country." From
this time onward, contemporary allusions and references in legal documents enable the scholar to
chart Shakespeare's career with greater accuracy
than is possible with most other Elizabethan dramatists.

By 1594 Shakespeare was a member of the company of actors known as the Lord Chamberlain's
Men. After the accession of James I, in 1603, the
company would have the sovereign for their patron
and would be known as the King's Men. During the
period of its greatest prosperity, this company
would have as its principal theatres the Globe and
the Blackfriars. Shakespeare was both an actor and
a shareholder in the company. Tradition has as-
signed him such acting roles as Adam in *As You
Like It* and the Ghost in *Hamlet,* a modest place

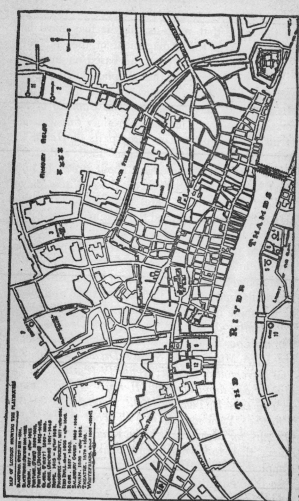

Map of London, showing the playhouses of Shakespeare's time. From J. Q. Adams, *Shakespearean Playhouses* (1917).

on the stage that suggests that he may have had
other duties in the management of the company.
Such conclusions, however, are based on surmise.

What we do know is that his plays were popular
and that he was highly successful in his vocation.
His first play may have been *The Comedy of Errors*, acted perhaps in 1591. Certainly this was one
of his earliest plays. The three parts of *Henry VI*
were acted sometime between 1590 and 1592.
Critics are not in agreement about precisely how
much Shakespeare wrote of these three plays.
Richard III probably dates from 1593. With this
play Shakespeare captured the imagination of Elizabethan audiences, then enormously interested in
historical plays. With *Richard III* Shakespeare also
gave an interpretation pleasing to the Tudors of the
rise to power of the grandfather of Queen Elizabeth.
From this time onward, Shakespeare's plays followed
on the stage in rapid succession: *Titus Andronicus,
The Taming of the Shrew, The Two Gentlemen of
Verona, Love's Labor's Lost, Romeo and Juliet, Richard II, A Midsummer Night's Dream, King John,
The Merchant of Venice, Henry IV (Parts 1 and 2),
Much Ado About Nothing, Henry V, Julius Cæsar,
As You Like It, Twelfth Night, Hamlet, The Merry
Wives of Windsor, All's Well That Ends Well,
Measure for Measure, Othello, King Lear*, and nine
others that followed before Shakespeare retired
completely, about 1613.

In the course of his career in London, he made
enough money to enable him to retire to Stratford
with a competence. His purchase on May 4, 1597,

of New Place, then the second-largest dwelling in Stratford, a "pretty house of brick and timber," with a handsome garden, indicates his increasing prosperity. There his wife and children lived while he busied himself in the London theatres. The summer before he acquired New Place, his life was darkened by the death of his only son, Hamnet, a child of eleven. In May, 1602, Shakespeare purchased one hundred and seven acres of fertile farmland near Stratford and a few months later bought a cottage and garden across the alley from New Place. About 1611, he seems to have returned permanently to Stratford, for the next year a legal document refers to him as "William Shakespeare of Stratford-upon-Avon . . . gentleman." To achieve the desired appellation of gentleman, William Shakespeare had seen to it that the College of Heralds in 1596 granted his father a coat of arms. In one step he thus became a second-generation gentleman.

Shakespeare's daughter Susanna made a good match in 1607 with Dr. John Hall, a prominent and prosperous Stratford physician. His second daughter, Judith, did not marry until she was thirty-two years old, and then, under somewhat scandalous circumstances, she married Thomas Quiney, a Stratford vintner. On March 25, 1616, Shakespeare made his will, bequeathing his landed property to Susanna, £300 to Judith, certain sums to other relatives, and his second-best bed to his wife, Anne. Much has been made of the second-best bed, but the legacy probably indicates only that Anne liked that particular bed. Shakespeare, following the practice of the time, may have already arranged with Susanna for his wife's care. Finally, on April 23, 1616, the anniversary of his birth, William Shakespeare died, and he was buried on April 25 within the chancel of Trinity Church, as befitted an honored citizen. On August 6, 1623, a few months before the publication of the collected edition of Shakespeare's plays, Anne Shakespeare joined her husband in death.

THE PUBLICATION OF HIS PLAYS

During his lifetime Shakespeare made no effort to publish any of his plays, though eighteen appeared in print in single-play editions known as quartos. Some of these are corrupt versions known as "bad quartos." No quarto, so far as is known, had the author's approval. Plays were not considered "literature" any more than most radio and television scripts today are considered literature. Dramatists sold their plays outright to the theatrical companies and it was usually considered in the company's interest to keep plays from getting into print. To achieve a reputation as a man of letters, Shakespeare wrote his *Sonnets* and his narrative poems, *Venus and Adonis* and *The Rape of Lucrece,* but he probably never dreamed that his plays would establish his reputation as a literary genius. Only Ben Jonson, a man known for his colossal conceit, had the crust to call his plays *Works,* as he did when he published an edition in 1616. But men laughed at Ben Jonson.

After Shakespeare's death, two of his old colleagues in the King's Men, John Heminges and Henry Condell, decided that it would be a good thing to print, in more accurate versions than were then available, the plays already published and eighteen additional plays not previously published in quarto. In 1623 appeared *Mr. William Shakespeares Comedies, Histories, & Tragedies. Published according to the True Originall Copies. London. Printed by Isaac Iaggard and Ed. Blount.* This was the famous First Folio, a work that had the authority of Shakespeare's associates. The only play commonly attributed to Shakespeare that was omitted in the First Folio was *Pericles*. In their preface, "To the great Variety of Readers," Heminges and Condell state that whereas "you were abused with diverse stolen and surreptitious copies, maimed and deformed by the frauds and stealths of injurious impostors that exposed them, even those are now offered to your view cured and perfect of their limbs; and all the rest, absolute in their numbers, as he conceived them." What they used for printer's copy is one of the vexed problems of scholarship, and skilled bibliographers have devoted years of study to the question of the relation of the "copy" for the First Folio to Shakespeare's manuscripts. In some cases it is clear that the editors corrected printed quarto versions of the plays, probably by comparison with playhouse scripts. Whether these scripts were in Shakespeare's autograph is anybody's guess. No manuscript of any play in Shakespeare's handwriting has survived. Indeed, very few play manuscripts from this period by any author are extant. The Tudor and Stuart periods had not yet learned to prize autographs and authors' original manuscripts.

Since the First Folio contains eighteen plays not previously printed, it is the only source for these. For the other eighteen, which had appeared in quarto versions, the First Folio also has the authority of an edition prepared and overseen by Shakespeare's colleagues and professional associates. But since editorial standards in 1623 were far from strict, and Heminges and Condell were actors rather than editors by profession, the texts are sometimes careless. The printing and proofreading of the First Folio also left much to be desired, and some garbled passages have had to be corrected and emended. The "good quarto" texts have to be taken into account in preparing a modern edition.

Because of the great popularity of Shakespeare through the centuries, the First Folio has become a prized book, but it is not a very rare one, for it is estimated that 238 copies are extant. The Folger Shakespeare Library in Washington, D.C., has seventy-nine copies of the First Folio, collected by the founder, Henry Clay Folger, who believed that a collation of as many texts as possible would reveal significant facts about the text of Shakespeare's plays. Dr. Charlton Hinman, using an ingenious machine of his own invention for mechanical collating, has made many discoveries that throw light on Shakespeare's text and on printing practices of the day.

The probability is that the First Folio of 1623 had an edition of between 1,000 and 1,250 copies. It is believed that it sold for £1, which made it an expensive book, for £1 in 1623 was equivalent to something between $40 and $50 in modern purchasing power.

During the seventeenth century, Shakespeare was sufficiently popular to warrant three later editions in folio size, the Second Folio of 1632, the Third Folio of 1663–1664, and the Fourth Folio of 1685. The Third Folio added six other plays ascribed to Shakespeare, but these are apocryphal.

THE SHAKESPEAREAN THEATRE

The theatres in which Shakespeare's plays were performed were vastly different from those we know today. The stage was a platform that jutted out into the area now occupied by the first rows of seats on the main floor, what is called the "orchestra" in America and the "pit" in England. This platform had no curtain to come down at the ends of acts and scenes. And although simple stage properties were available, the Elizabethan theatre lacked both the machinery and the elaborate movable scenery of the modern theatre. In the rear of the platform stage was a curtained area that could be used as an inner room, a tomb, or any such scene that might be required. A balcony above this inner room, and perhaps balconies on the sides of the stage, could represent the upper deck of a ship, the entry to Juliet's room, or a prison window. A trap door in the stage provided an entrance for ghosts and devils from the nether regions, and a similar trap in the canopied structure over the stage, known as the "heavens," made it possible to let down angels on a rope. These primitive stage arrangements help to account for many elements in Elizabethan plays. For example, since there was no curtain, the dramatist frequently felt the necessity of writing into his play action to clear the stage at the ends of acts and scenes. The funeral march at the end of *Hamlet* is not there merely for atmosphere; Shakespeare had to get the corpses off the stage. The lack of scenery also freed the dramatist from undue concern about the exact location of his sets, and the physical relation of his various settings to each other did not have to be worked out with the same precision as in the modern theatre.

Before London had buildings designed exclusively for theatrical entertainment, plays were given in inns and taverns. The characteristic inn of the period had an inner courtyard with rooms opening onto balconies overlooking the yard. Players could set up their temporary stages at one end of the yard and audiences could find seats on the balconies out of the weather. The poorer sort could stand or sit on the cobblestones in the yard, which was open to the sky. The first theatres followed this construction, and throughout the Elizabethan period the large public theatres had a yard in front of the stage open to the weather, with two or three tiers of covered balconies extending around the theatre. This physical structure again influenced the writing of

The Globe Playhouse.
From Visscher's *View of London* (1616).

plays. Because a dramatist wanted the actors to be heard, he frequently wrote into his play orations that could be delivered with declamatory effect. He also provided spectacle, buffoonery, and broad jests to keep the riotous groundlings in the yard entertained and quiet.

In another respect the Elizabethan theatre differed greatly from ours. It had no actresses. All women's roles were taken by boys, sometimes recruited from the boys' choirs of the London churches. Some of these youths acted their roles with great skill and the Elizabethans did not seem to be aware of any incongruity. The first actresses on the professional English stage appeared after the Restoration of Charles II, in 1660, when exiled Englishmen brought back from France practices of the French stage.

London in the Elizabethan period, as now, was the center of theatrical interest, though wandering actors from time to time traveled through the country performing in inns, halls, and the houses of the nobility. The first professional playhouse, called simply The Theatre, was erected by James Burbage, father of Shakespeare's colleague Richard Burbage, in 1576 on lands of the old Holywell Priory adjacent to Finsbury Fields, a playground and park area just north of the city walls. It had the advantage of being outside the city's jurisdiction and yet was near enough to be easily accessible. Soon after The Theatre was opened, another playhouse called The Curtain was erected in the same neighborhood. Both of these playhouses had open courtyards and were probably polygonal in shape.

About the time The Curtain opened, Richard Farrant, Master of the Children of the Chapel Royal at Windsor and of St. Paul's, conceived the idea of opening a "private" theatre in the old monastery buildings of the Blackfriars, not far from St. Paul's Cathedral in the heart of the city. This theatre was ostensibly to train the choirboys in plays for presentation at court, but Farrant managed to present plays to paying audiences and achieved considerable success until aristocratic neighbors complained and had the theatre closed. This first Blackfriars Theatre was significant, however, because it popularized the boy actors in a professional way and it paved the way for a second theatre in the Blackfriars, which Shakespeare's company took over more than thirty years later. By the last years of the sixteenth century, London had at least six professional theatres and still others were erected during the reign of James I.

The Globe Theatre, the playhouse that most people connect with Shakespeare, was erected early in 1599 on the Bankside, the area across the Thames from the city. Its construction had a dramatic beginning, for on the night of December 28, 1598, James Burbage's sons, Cuthbert and Richard, gathered together a crew who tore down the old theatre in Holywell and carted the timbers across the river to a site that they had chosen for a new playhouse. The reason for this clandestine operation was a row with the landowner over the lease to the

Holywell property. The site chosen for the Globe
was another playground outside of the city's jurisdiction, a region of somewhat unsavory character.
Not far away was the Bear Garden, an amphi-
theatre devoted to the baiting of bears and bulls.
This was also the region occupied by many houses
of ill fame licensed by the Bishop of Winchester
and the source of substantial revenue to him. But it
was easily accessible either from London Bridge
or by means of the cheap boats operated by the
London watermen, and it had the great advantage
of being beyond the authority of the Puritanical
aldermen of London, who frowned on plays because they lured apprentices from work, filled their
heads with improper ideas, and generally exerted
a bad influence. The aldermen also complained that
the crowds drawn together in the theatre helped
to spread the plague.

The Globe was the handsomest theatre up to its
time. It was a large building, apparently octagonal
in shape, and open like its predecessors to the sky
in the center, but capable of seating a large audience in its covered balconies. To erect and operate
the Globe, the Burbages organized a syndicate
composed of the leading members of the dramatic
company, of which Shakespeare was a member.
Since it was open to the weather and depended on
natural light, plays had to be given in the afternoon.
This caused no hardship in the long afternoons of
an English summer, but in the winter the weather
was a great handicap and discouraged all except
the hardiest. For that reason, in 1608 Shakespeare's

company was glad to take over the lease of the second Blackfriars Theatre, a substantial, roomy hall reconstructed within the framework of the old monastery building. This theatre was protected from the weather and its stage was artificially lighted by chandeliers of candles. This became the winter playhouse for Shakespeare's company and at once proved so popular that the congestion of traffic created an embarrassing problem. Stringent regulations had to be made for the movement of coaches in the vicinity. Shakespeare's company continued to use the Globe during the summer months. In 1613 a squib fired from a cannon during a performance of *Henry VIII* fell on the thatched roof and the Globe burned to the ground. The next year it was rebuilt.

London had other famous theatres. The Rose, just west of the Globe, was built by Philip Henslowe, a semiliterate denizen of the Bankside, who became one of the most important theatrical owners and producers of the Tudor and Stuart periods. What is more important for historians, he kept a detailed account book, which provides much of our information about theatrical history in his time. Another famous theatre on the Bankside was the Swan, which a Dutch priest, Johannes de Witt, visited in 1596. The crude drawing of the stage which he made was copied by his friend Arend van Buchell; it is one of the important pieces of contemporary evidence for theatrical construction. Among the other theatres, the Fortune, north of the city, on Golding Lane, and the Red Bull, even farther away

testum

spectra

porticus

orchestra

mimorum ædes

ingressus

proscænium

planties siue arena

xumtum ʃed viʃerio et ʃecundum, biʃʃeracum conʃtabit
hui xplinatum, in quo multi verʃi. tauri St ʃtupenda
magnitudinis vanes, Dʃtutib canus I ʃeptis alluntur, qui
laud

Interior of the Swan Theatre.
From a drawing by Johannes de Witt (1596).

from the city, off St. John's Street, were the most popular. The Red Bull, much frequented by apprentices, favored sensational and sometimes rowdy plays.

The actors who kept all of these theatres going were organized into companies under the protection of some noble patron. Traditionally actors had enjoyed a low reputation. In some of the ordinances they were classed as vagrants; in the phraseology of the time, "rogues, vagabonds, sturdy beggars, and common players" were all listed together as undesirables. To escape penalties often meted out to these characters, organized groups of actors managed to gain the protection of various personages of high degree. In the later years of Elizabeth's reign, a group flourished under the name of the Queen's Men; another group had the protection of the Lord Admiral and were known as the Lord Admiral's Men. Edward Alleyn, son-in-law of Philip Henslowe, was the leading spirit in the Lord Admiral's Men. Besides the adult companies, troupes of boy actors from time to time also enjoyed considerable popularity. Among these were the Children of Paul's and the Children of the Chapel Royal.

The company with which Shakespeare had a long association had for its first patron Henry Carey, Lord Hunsdon, the Lord Chamberlain, and hence they were known as the Lord Chamberlain's Men. After the accession of James I, they became the King's Men. This company was the great rival of the Lord Admiral's Men, managed by Henslowe and Alleyn.

All was not easy for the players in Shakespeare's time, for the aldermen of London were always eager for an excuse to close up the Blackfriars and any other theatres in their jurisdiction. The theatres outside the jurisdiction of London were not immune from interference, for they might be shut up by order of the Privy Council for meddling in politics or for various other offenses, or they might be closed in time of plague lest they spread infection. During plague times, the actors usually went on tour and played the provinces wherever they could find an audience. Particularly frightening were the plagues of 1592–1594 and 1613 when the theatres closed and the players, like many other Londoners, had to take to the country.

Though players had a low social status, they enjoyed great popularity, and one of the favorite forms of entertainment at court was the performance of plays. To be commanded to perform at court conferred great prestige upon a company of players, and printers frequently noted that fact when they published plays. Several of Shakespeare's plays were performed before the sovereign, and Shakespeare himself undoubtedly acted in some of these plays.

REFERENCES FOR FURTHER READING

Many readers will want suggestions for further reading about Shakespeare and his times. The literature in this field is enormous but a few references will serve as guides to further study. A simple and useful little book is Gerald Sanders, *A Shakespeare Primer* (New York, 1950). *A Companion to Shakespeare Studies,* edited by Harley Granville-Barker and G. B. Harrison (Cambridge, 1934) is a valuable guide. More detailed but still not so voluminous as to be confusing is Hazelton Spencer, *The Art and Life of William Shakespeare* (New York, 1940) which, like Sanders' handbook, contains a brief annotated list of useful books on various aspects of the subject. The most detailed and scholarly work providing complete factual information about Shakespeare is Sir Edmund Chambers, *William Shakespeare: A Study of Facts and Problems* (2 vols., Oxford, 1930). For detailed, factual information about the Elizabethan and seventeenth-century stages, the definitive reference works are Sir Edmund Chambers, *The Elizabethan Stage* (4 vols., Oxford, 1923) and Gerald E. Bentley, *The Jacobean and Caroline Stage* (5 vols., Oxford, 1941–1956). Alfred Harbage, *Shakespeare's Audience* (New York, 1941) throws light on the nature and tastes of the customers for whom Elizabethan dramatists wrote.

Although specialists disagree about the details of stage construction, the reader will find essential information in John C. Adams, *The Globe Playhouse: Its Design and Equipment* (Cambridge, Mass., 1942). A model of the Globe playhouse by Dr. Adams is on permanent exhibition in the Folger Shakespeare Library in Washington, D.C. An excellent description of the architecture of the Globe is Irwin Smith, *Shakespeare's Globe Playhouse: A Modern Reconstruction in Text and Scale Drawings Based upon the Reconstruction of the Globe by John Cranford Adams* (New York, 1956). Another recent study of the physical characteristics of the Globe is C. Walter Hodges, *The Globe Restored* (London, 1953). An easily read history of the early theatres is J. Q. Adams, *Shakespearean Playhouses: A History of English Theatres from the Beginnings to the Restoration* (Boston, 1917).

The following titles on theatrical history will provide information about Shakespeare's plays in later periods: Alfred Harbage, *Theatre for Shakespeare* (Toronto, 1955); Esther Cloudman Dunn, *Shakespeare in America* (New York, 1939); George C. D. Odell, *Shakespeare from Betterton to Irving* (2 vols., London, 1931); Arthur Colby Sprague, *Shakespeare and the Actors: The Stage Business in His Plays* (*1660–1905*) (Cambridge, Mass., 1944) and *Shakespearian Players and Performances* (Cambridge, Mass., 1953); Leslie Hotson, *The Commonwealth and Restoration Stage* (Cambridge, Mass., 1928); Alwin Thaler, *Shakespere to Sheridan: A Book About the Theatre of Yesterday and To-day* (Cambridge, Mass., 1922); Ernest Bradlee Watson, *Sheridan to Robertson: A Study of the 19th-Century*

London Stage (Cambridge, Mass., 1926). Enid Welsford, *The Court Masque* (Cambridge, Mass., 1927) is an excellent study of the characteristics of this form of entertainment.

Harley Granville-Barker, *Prefaces to Shakespeare* (5 vols., London, 1927–1948) provides stimulating critical discussion of the plays. An older classic of criticism is Andrew C. Bradley, *Shakespearean Tragedy: Lectures on Hamlet, Othello, King Lear, Macbeth* (London, 1904), which is now available in an inexpensive reprint (New York, 1955). Thomas M. Parrot, *Shakespearean Comedy* (New York, 1949) is scholarly and readable. Shakespeare's dramatizations of English history are examined in E. M. W. Tillyard, *Shakespeare's History Plays* (London, 1948), and Lily Bess Campbell, *Shakespeare's "Histories," Mirrors of Elizabethan Policy* (San Marino, Calif., 1947) contains a more technical discussion of the same subject.

In *The Hollow Crown: A Life of Richard II* (New York, 1961), Harold F. Hutchison places this sovereign in perspective as a medieval figure instead of the Tudor prince portrayed by Shakespeare. He shows that many of the persons around Richard, including Bushy, Green, and Bagot, were not the wastrels that the Lancastrian chroniclers and Shakespeare made them out. This biography might well be read to provide a contrasting picture to the one that Shakespeare drew. The introduction to the new Arden edition of *Richard II*, edited by Peter Ure (Cambridge, Mass., 1956) provides a succinct and sensible summary of recent scholarship on this play, including an excellent discussion of the sources. The introduction to John Dover Wilson's new Cambridge edition (Cambridge, 1939) is provocative even if it is not convincing about Shakespeare's reworking of an old play. The use that Shakespeare probably made of the old play *Thomas of Woodstock* is treated by A. P. Rossiter in the introduction to his edition, which he entitled *Woodstock: A Moral History* (London, 1946). Valuable insights into Shakespeare's historical point of view and purpose will be found in Lily Bess Campbell, *Shakespeare's "Histories": Mirrors of Elizabethan Policy* (San Marino, Calif., 1947), *passim*. For a contention that Shakespeare worked away at his sources like a research scholar, see Matthew W. Black, "The Sources of Shakespeare's *Richard II*," in *Joseph Quincy Adams Memorial Studies* (Washington, 1948), pp. 199–216. The facsimile edition of the third quarto of 1598, edited by A. W. Pollard (London, 1916) provides an introduction giving a detailed account of the relationship between the various quartos.

The question of the authenticity of Shakespeare's plays arouses perennial attention. A book that demolishes the notion of hidden cryptograms in the plays is William F. Friedman and Elizebeth S. Friedman, *The Shakespearean Ciphers Examined* (New York, 1957). A succinct account of the various absurdities advanced to suggest the authorship of a multitude of candidates other than Shakespeare will be found in R. C. Churchill's *Shakespeare and His Betters* (Bloomington, Ind., 1959) and Frank W.

Wadsworth, *The Poacher from Stratford: A Partial Account of the Controversy over the Authorship of Shakespeare's Plays* (Berkeley, Calif., 1958). An essay on the curious notions in the writings of the anti-Shakespeareans is that by Louis B. Wright, "The Anti-Shakespeare Industry and the Growth of Cults," *The Virginia Quarterly Review*, XXXV (1959), pp. 289–303. Another recent discussion of the subject, *The Authorship of Shakespeare*, by James G. McManaway (Washington, 1962), presents all the evidence from contemporary records to prove the identity of Shakespeare the actor-playwright with Shakespeare of Stratford.

Reprints of some of the sources of Shakespeare's plays can be found in *Shakespeare's Library* (2 vols., 1850), edited by John Payne Collier, and *The Shakespeare Classics* (12 vols., 1907–1926), edited by Israel Gollancz. Geoffrey Bullough, *Narrative and Dramatic Sources of Shakespeare* is a new series of volumes reprinting the sources. Four volumes covering the early comedies, comedies (1597–1603), and histories are now available. For discussion of Shakespeare's use of his sources see Kenneth Muir, *Shakespeare's Sources: Comedies and Tragedies* (London, 1957). Thomas M. Cranfill has recently edited a facsimile reprint of *Riche His Farewell to Military Profession* (1581), which contains stories that Shakespeare probably used for several of his plays.

Interesting pictures as well as new information about Shakespeare will be found in F. E. Halliday, *Shakespeare, a Pictorial Biography* (London, 1956).

Allardyce Nicoll, *The Elizabethans* (Cambridge, 1957) contains a variety of illustrations.

A brief, clear, and accurate account of Tudor history is S. T. Bindoff, *The Tudors*, in the Penguin series. A readable general history is G. M. Trevelyan, *The History of England,* first published in 1926 and available in many editions. G. M. Trevelyan, *English Social History,* first published in 1942 and also available in many editions, provides fascinating information about England in all periods. Sir John Neale, *Queen Elizabeth* (London, 1934) is the best study of the great Queen. Various aspects of life in the Elizabethan period are treated in Louis B. Wright, *Middle-Class Culture in Elizabethan England* (Chapel Hill, N.C., 1935: reprinted, Ithaca, N.Y., 1958). *Shakespeare's England: An Account of the Life and Manners of His Age,* edited by Sidney Lee and C. T. Onions (2 vols., Oxford, 1916), provides a large amount of information on many aspects of life in the Elizabethan period. Additional information will be found in Muriel St. C. Byrne, *Elizabethan Life in Town and Country* (London, 1925; rev. ed., 1954; Paperback, N.Y., 1961).

The Folger Shakespeare Library is currently publishing a series of illustrated pamphlets on various aspects of English life in the sixteenth and seventeenth centuries. The following titles are available: Dorothy E. Mason, *Music in Elizabethan England;* Craig R. Thompson, *The English Church in the Sixteenth Century;* Louis B. Wright, *Shakespeare's Theatre and the Dramatic Tradition;* Giles E. Dawson, *The Life of William Shakespeare;* Virginia A. LaMar, *English Dress in the Age of Shakespeare;* Craig R. Thompson, *The Bible in English, 1525–1611;* Craig R. Thompson, *Schools in Tudor England;* Craig R. Thompson, *Universities in Tudor England;* Lilly C. Stone, *English Sports and Recreations;* Conyers Read, *The Government of England under Elizabeth;* Virginia A. LaMar, *Travel and Roads in England;* John R. Hale, *The Art of War and Renaissance England;* and Albert J. Schmidt, *The Yeoman in Tudor and Stuart England.*

[Dramatis Personae

King Richard II.
John of Gaunt, Duke of Lancaster, } uncles to the King.
Edmund of Langley, Duke of York, }
Henry, surnamed Bolingbroke, Duke of Hereford, son to
    John of Gaunt; afterward King Henry IV.
Duke of Aumerle, son of the Duke of York.
Thomas Mowbray, Duke of Norfolk.
Duke of Surrey.
Earl of Salisbury.
Lord Berkeley
Bushy, }
Bagot, } servants to King Richard.
Green, }
Earl of Northumberland.
Henry Percy, surnamed Hotspur, his son.
Lord Ross.
Lord Willoughby.
Lord Fitzwater.
Bishop of Carlisle.
Abbot of Westminster.
Lord Marshal.
Sir Stephen Scroop.
Sir Pierce of Exton.
Captain of a band of Welshmen.
Queen to King Richard.   Duchess of Gloucester.
Duchess of York.   Ladies attending the Queen.
Lords, Heralds, Officers, Soldiers, Gardeners, Messen-
    gers, Keeper, Groom, and other Attendants.

SCENE: *England and Wales.*]

THE TRAGEDY OF
RICHARD
THE SECOND

ACT I

I. i. Henry, Duke of Hereford, and Thomas Mowbray, Duke of Norfolk, have been summoned by King Richard to particularize their mutual accusations of treason. Hereford accuses Norfolk of the murder of the Duke of Gloucester, the misuse of funds entrusted to him for the pay of troops, and complicity in treasonous plots against the King. Each lord challenges the other to combat to prove the truth of their accusations. When the King is unable to reconcile them he orders them to appear for the combat at Coventry on St. Lambert's Day.

<hr/>

1. **Gaunt:** i.e., Ghent, birthplace of John, Duke of Lancaster.

2. **band:** bond.

3. **Hereford:** Henry, also known as "Bolingbroke," from his birthplace, held the title of Duke of Hereford.

4. **make good:** prove; **boist'rous:** rude; rough; **late appeal:** recent accusation.

5. **our . . . us:** the royal plural; **leisure:** lack of leisure.

9. **ancient malice:** personal enmity of long standing.

10. **worthily:** justly.

13. **apparent:** obvious; undoubted.

ACT I

Scene I. [London. The Palace.]

Enter King Richard, John of Gaunt, with other Nobles
and Attendants.

King. Old John of Gaunt, time-honored Lancaster,
Hast thou, according to thy oath and band,
Brought hither Henry Hereford, thy bold son,
Here to make good the boist'rous late appeal,
Which then our leisure would not let us hear,   5
Against the Duke of Norfolk, Thomas Mowbray?
Gaunt. I have, my liege.
King. Tell me, moreover, hast thou sounded him
If he appeal the Duke on ancient malice,
Or worthily, as a good subject should,   10
On some known ground of treachery in him?
Gaunt. As near as I could sift him on that argument,
On some apparent danger seen in him
Aimed at your Highness, no inveterate malice.
King. Then call them to our presence.   15
                              [*Exit Attendant.*]
                              Face to face,
And frowning brow to brow, ourselves will hear

I

19. **High-stomached:** proud and testy. "Stomach" meant both "courage" and "resentment."

24. **hap:** fortune.

33. **Tend'ring:** cherishing.

35. **appellant:** one who accuses another of treason.

40. **miscreant:** faithless villain.

41. **good:** highborn.

44. **note:** stigma.

Richard II.
From John Taylor, *All the Works* (1630).

The accuser and the accused freely speak.
High-stomached are they both and full of ire,
In rage deaf as the sea, hasty as fire.   20

Enter Bolingbroke and Mowbray.

Boling. Many years of happy days befall
My gracious sovereign, my most loving liege!
  Mowb. Each day still better other's happiness
Until the heavens, envying earth's good hap,
Add an immortal title to your crown!   25
  King. We thank you both. Yet one but flatters us,
As well appeareth by the cause you come,
Namely, to appeal each other of high treason.
Cousin of Hereford, what dost thou object
Against the Duke of Norfolk, Thomas Mowbray?   30
  Boling. First—heaven be the record to my speech!—
In the devotion of a subject's love,
Tend'ring the precious safety of my prince
And free from other misbegotten hate,
Come I appellant to this princely presence.   35
Now, Thomas Mowbray, do I turn to thee,
And mark my greeting well; for what I speak
My body shall make good upon this earth
Or my divine soul answer it in heaven.
Thou art a traitor and a miscreant,   40
Too good to be so, and too bad to live,
Since the more fair and crystal is the sky,
The uglier seem the clouds that in it fly.
Once more, the more to aggravate the note,

47. **right-drawn:** righteously drawn.

51. **eager:** sharp.

58. **post:** ride posthaste.

65. **tied:** obliged.

67. **inhabitable:** uninhabitable, from Latin *inhabitabilis*.

72. **gage:** pledge—often a glove.

Taking up the gage.
From Olaus Magnus, *Historia de gentibus septentrionalibus* (1555).

With a foul traitor's name stuff I thy throat   45
And wish (so please my sovereign), ere I move,
What my tongue speaks, my right-drawn sword may
     prove.
    Mowb. Let not my cold words here accuse my zeal.
'Tis not the trial of a woman's war,   50
The bitter clamor of two eager tongues,
Can arbitrate this cause betwixt us twain;
The blood is hot that must be cooled for this.
Yet can I not of such tame patience boast
As to be hushed and naught at all to say.   55
First, the fair reverence of your Highness curbs me
From giving reins and spurs to my free speech,
Which else would post until it had returned
These terms of treason doubled down his throat.
Setting aside his high blood's royalty,   60
And let him be no kinsman to my liege,
I do defy him and I spit at him,
Call him a slanderous coward and a villain;
Which to maintain, I would allow him odds
And meet him, were I tied to run afoot   65
Even to the frozen ridges of the Alps,
Or any other ground inhabitable
Where ever Englishman durst set his foot.
Meantime let this defend my loyalty—
By all my hopes, most falsely doth he lie.   70
    Boling. Pale trembling coward, there I throw my
     gage,
Disclaiming here the kindred of the King,
And lay aside my high blood's royalty,

75. **fear, not reverence, makes thee to except:** i.e., fear of me, not reverence for the King, causes you to set aside.

77. **mine honor's pawn:** i.e., the gage.

83-4. **in any fair degree/Or chivalrous design of knightly trial:** i.e., in a manner appropriate to our rank and the laws of chivalrous combat.

89. **inherit us:** cause us to have.

91. **Look what:** a sixteenth-century idiom meaning "whatever."

93. **nobles:** gold coins worth 6s. 8d. each.

94. **in name of lendings:** on the pretext of advancing that sum to pay soldiers.

95. **lewd:** low; ignoble.

100. **these eighteen years:** i.e., since Wat Tyler's rebellion in 1381; the present year is 1398. Holinshed includes this charge in Hereford's accusation of Norfolk.

102. **head:** source.

Which fear, not reverence, makes thee to except.   75
If guilty dread have left thee so much strength
As to take up mine honor's pawn, then stoop.
By that and all the rites of knighthood else,
Will I make good against thee, arm to arm,
What I have spoke or thou canst worse devise.   80
   Mowb. I take it up; and by that sword I swear
Which gently laid my knighthood on my shoulder,
I'll answer thee in any fair degree
Or chivalrous design of knightly trial;
And when I mount, alive may I not light   85
If I be traitor or unjustly fight!
   King. What doth our cousin lay to Mowbray's
     charge?
It must be great that can inherit us
So much as of a thought of ill in him.   90
   Boling. Look what I speak, my life shall prove it
     true—
That Mowbray hath received eight thousand nobles
In name of lendings for your Highness' soldiers,
The which he hath detained for lewd employments,   95
Like a false traitor and injurious villain.
Besides I say, and will in battle prove—
Or here, or elsewhere to the furthest verge
That ever was surveyed by English eye—
That all the treasons for these eighteen years   100
Complotted and contrived in this land
Fetch from false Mowbray their first head and spring.
Further I say, and further will maintain
Upon his bad life to make all this good,

105. **the Duke of Gloucester's death:** Gloucester died in prison at Calais in 1397 while in Norfolk's custody. The King approved of his death if he did not actually order it and historically Gloucester was under arrest for treason. Holinshed reports that he was smothered with a featherbed, but Shakespeare twice in the play implies that he was beheaded.

106. **Suggest:** incite; **soon-believing:** credulous.

114. **pitch:** the highest point of a hawk's flight.

118. **slander:** disgrace.

123. **scepter's awe:** the awe my scepter should command.

125. **partialize:** prejudice.

134. **For that:** because.

That he did plot the Duke of Gloucester's death,   105
Suggest his soon-believing adversaries,
And consequently, like a traitor coward,
Sluiced out his innocent soul through streams of blood;
Which blood, like sacrificing Abel's, cries,
Even from the tongueless caverns of the earth,   110
To me for justice and rough chastisement;
And, by the glorious worth of my descent,
This arm shall do it, or this life be spent.

  King. How high a pitch his resolution soars!
Thomas of Norfolk, what sayst thou to this?   115

  Mowb. O, let my sovereign turn away his face
And bid his ears a little while be deaf,
Till I have told this slander of his blood
How God and good men hate so foul a liar!

  King. Mowbray, impartial are our eyes and ears.   120
Were he my brother, nay, my kingdom's heir,
As he is but my father's brother's son,
Now by my scepter's awe I make a vow,
Such neighbor nearness to our sacred blood
Should nothing privilege him nor partialize   125
The unstooping firmness of my upright soul.
He is our subject, Mowbray; so art thou:
Free speech and fearless I to thee allow.

  Mowb. Then, Bolingbroke, as low as to thy heart
Through the false passage of thy throat, thou liest!   130
Three parts of that receipt I had for Calais
Disbursed I duly to His Highness' soldiers.
The other part reserved I by consent,
For that my sovereign liege was in my debt

135. **Upon remainder of a dear account:** against the balance of a heavy debt.

136. **his queen:** Richard's second wife, Isabel, daughter of Charles VI, King of France.

139. **Neglected my sworn duty in that case:** Holinshed reports that Norfolk delayed carrying out the King's orders to have Gloucester executed.

149. **recreant:** faithless wretch.

151. **interchangeably:** in reciprocation.

155. **In haste whereof:** i.e., in order to speedily prove my position.

Upon remainder of a dear account   135
Since last I went to France to fetch his queen.
Now swallow down that lie! For Gloucester's death,
I slew him not, but, to my own disgrace,
Neglected my sworn duty in that case.
For you, my noble Lord of Lancaster,   140
The honorable father to my foe,
Once did I lay an ambush for your life,
A trespass that doth vex my grieved soul;
But ere I last received the sacrament,
I did confess it and exactly begged   145
Your Grace's pardon, and I hope I had it.
This is my fault. As for the rest appealed,
It issues from the rancor of a villain,
A recreant and most degenerate traitor;
Which in myself I boldly will defend,   150
And interchangeably hurl down my gage
Upon this overweening traitor's foot
To prove myself a loyal gentleman
Even in the best blood chambered in his bosom.
In haste whereof most heartily I pray   155
Your Highness to assign our trial day.
   King. Wrath-kindled gentlemen, be ruled by me;
Let's purge this choler without letting blood.
This we prescribe, though no physician;
Deep malice makes too deep incision.   160
Forget, forgive; conclude and be agreed;
Our doctors say this is no month to bleed.
Good uncle, let this end where it begun;
We'll calm the Duke of Norfolk, you your son.

168. **When:** i.e., when will you do as I ask.

170–71. **There is no boot:** refusal is of no avail.

174. **name:** reputation.

175. **upon my grave:** engraved on my tomb.

177. **impeached:** impugned; **baffled:** disgraced, usually applied specifically to stripping a knight of the symbols of knighthood.

180. **breathed:** uttered; voiced.

182. **Lions make leopards tame:** a reference to the heraldic devices of the King and Norfolk. Richard's royal lion is mightier than Norfolk's leopard (the heraldic term for a lion in any position other than rampant).

186. **mortal times:** the earthly lives of humans.

Gaunt. To be a make-peace shall become my age. 165
Throw down, my son, the Duke of Norfolk's gage.
　　King. And, Norfolk, throw down his.
　　Gaunt.　　　　　　　　When, Harry? when?
Obedience bids I should not bid again.
　　King. Norfolk, throw down, we bid. There is no 170
　　　boot.
　　Mowb. Myself I throw, dread sovereign, at thy foot.
My life thou shalt command, but not my shame.
The one my duty owes; but my fair name,
Despite of death, that lives upon my grave, 175
To dark dishonor's use thou shalt not have.
I am disgraced, impeached, and baffled here;
Pierced to the soul with slander's venomed spear,
The which no balm can cure but his heartblood
Which breathed this poison. 180
　　King.　　　　　　　Rage must be withstood.
Give me his gage. Lions make leopards tame.
　　Mowb. Yea, but not change his spots! Take but my
　　　shame,
And I resign my gage. My dear dear lord, 185
The purest treasure mortal times afford
Is spotless reputation. That away,
Men are but gilded loam or painted clay.
A jewel in a ten times barred-up chest
Is a bold spirit in a loyal breast. 190
Mine honor is my life. Both grow in one;
Take honor from me, and my life is done.
Then, dear my liege, mine honor let me try;
In that I live, and for that will I die.

198. **impeach my height:** discredit my loftiness; disgrace my birth.

199. **outdared:** daunted; cowed.

200. **such feeble wrong:** that is, the act of weakly apologizing to Norfolk and retracting his own accusations.

201. **sound . . . a parle:** signal a willingness to make peace.

202. **motive:** moving organ—his tongue.

203. **in his high disgrace:** greatly disgraced as it (the tongue) is.

208. **St. Lambert's Day:** September 17.

211. **atone:** reconcile.

212. **design the victor's chivalry:** so direct the contest that the man in the right will be the victor.

213. **Lord Marshal:** Thomas Holland, Duke of Surrey, appointed by King Richard to replace Norfolk, former Lord Marshal.

214. **home alarms:** domestic combats.

I. ii. Gloucester's widow reproaches his brother, John of Gaunt, for failing to avenge his death. Gaunt replies that since the King, the deputy of the Lord, is responsible, it is up to God alone to punish Gloucester's death if it was contrary to His law.

1. **part:** share; Thomas of Woodstock, the Duke of Gloucester, was Gaunt's brother.

King. Cousin, throw up your gage. Do you begin.   195
Boling. O, God defend my soul from such deep sin!
Shall I seem crestfallen in my father's sight?
Or with pale beggar-fear impeach my height
Before this outdared dastard? Ere my tongue
Shall wound my honor with such feeble wrong   200
Or sound so base a parle, my teeth shall tear
The slavish motive of recanting fear
And spit it bleeding in his high disgrace,
Where shame doth harbor, even in Mowbray's face.
                                        Exit Gaunt.

King. We were not born to sue, but to command;   205
Which since we cannot do to make you friends,
Be ready, as your lives shall answer it,
At Coventry upon St. Lambert's Day.
There shall your swords and lance arbitrate
The swelling difference of your settled hate: 210
Since we cannot atone you, we shall see
Justice design the victor's chivalry.
Lord Marshal, command our officers-at-arms
Be ready to direct these home alarms.
                                        Exeunt.

Scene II. [London, The Duke of Lancaster's Palace.]

Enter John of Gaunt with the Duchess of Gloucester.

Gaunt. Alas, the part I had in Woodstock's blood
Doth more solicit me than your exclaims
To stir against the butchers of his life!

4. **those hands:** the hands of the King.

11. **Edward:** Edward III.

15. **Destinies:** three Fates, goddesses of classical mythology, one of whom spun the thread of human destiny, while another determined its length and the third cut it.

21. **envy's:** malice's.

23. **metal:** substance; **self:** same.

28. **the model of thy father's life:** thy father's image.

30. **suff'ring:** permitting.

The three fates.
Vincenzo Cartari, *Imagini delli dei de gl'antichi* (1674).

But since correction lieth in those hands
Which made the fault that we cannot correct, 5
Put we our quarrel to the will of heaven,
Who, when they see the hours ripe on earth,
Will rain hot vengeance on offenders' heads.
    Duch. Finds brotherhood in thee no sharper spur?
Hath love in thy old blood no living fire? 10
Edward's seven sons, whereof thyself art one,
Were as seven vials of his sacred blood,
Or seven fair branches springing from one root.
Some of those seven are dried by nature's course,
Some of those branches by the Destinies cut; 15
But Thomas, my dear lord, my life, my Gloucester,
One vial full of Edward's sacred blood,
One flourishing branch of his most royal root,
Is cracked, and all the precious liquor spilt,
Is hacked down, and his summer leaves all faded, 20
By envy's hand and murder's bloody ax.
Ah, Gaunt, his blood was thine! That bed, that womb,
That metal, that self mold that fashioned thee,
Made him a man; and though thou livest and breathest,
Yet art thou slain in him. Thou dost consent 25
In some large measure to thy father's death
In that thou seest thy wretched brother die,
Who was the model of thy father's life.
Call it not patience, Gaunt; it is despair.
In suff'ring thus thy brother to be slaught'red 30
Thou showest the naked pathway to thy life,
Teaching stern murder how to butcher thee.
That which in mean men we entitle patience

38. **His deputy:** the King.

46. **fell:** fierce.

49. **career:** assault. A **career** is literally a horse's charge at full speed.

53. **caitiff recreant:** captive coward.

54. **sometimes:** former.

55. **With . . . Grief, must end her life:** i.e., her grief will endure as long as she lives.

63. **Commend me:** give my greetings; **Edmund York:** Edmund of Langley, Duke of York.

Is pale cold cowardice in noble breasts.
What shall I say? To safeguard thine own life,   35
The best way is to venge my Gloucester's death.
 Gaunt. God's is the quarrel; for God's substitute,
His deputy anointed in His sight,
Hath caused his death; the which if wrongfully,
Let heaven revenge; for I may never lift   40
An angry arm against His minister.
 Duch. Where then, alas, may I complain myself?
 Gaunt. To God, the widow's champion and defense.
 Duch. Why then, I will. Farewell, old Gaunt.
Thou goest to Coventry, there to behold   45
Our cousin Hereford and fell Mowbray fight.
O, sit my husband's wrongs on Hereford's spear,
That it may enter butcher Mowbray's breast!
Or, if misfortune miss the first career,
Be Mowbray's sins so heavy in his bosom   50
That they may break his foaming courser's back
And throw the rider headlong in the lists,
A caitiff recreant to my cousin Hereford!
Farewell, old Gaunt. Thy sometimes brother's wife
With her companion, Grief, must end her life.   55
 Gaunt. Sister, farewell; I must to Coventry.
As much good stay with thee as go with me!
 Duch. Yet one word more! Grief boundeth where
  it falls,
Not with the empty hollowness, but weight.   60
I take my leave before I have begun,
For sorrow ends not when it seemeth done.
Commend me to thy brother, Edmund York.

67. **Plashy:** Pleshey, Essex, the Duke of Gloucester's country home.

70. **Unpeopled offices:** servantless service rooms (kitchens, etc.).

||||||||||||||||||||||||||||||||||||||||||||||||||||||||||||

I. iii. Hereford and Norfolk meet on the appointed day and repeat their accusations. When they are about to fight the King halts the proceedings and, after consultation with his Council, orders them both banished—Hereford for ten years, which he reduces to six years in compassion for Gaunt's grief, and Norfolk for life.

||||||||||||||||||||||||||||||||||||||

2. **at all points:** completely.
3. **sprightfully and bold:** spiritedly and boldly.
4. **Stays:** awaits.

Lo, this is all. Nay, yet depart not so!
Though this be all, do not so quickly go.   65
  shall remember more. Bid him—ah, what?—
  Vith all good speed at Plashy visit me.
  lack, and what shall good old York there see
  But empty lodgings and unfurnished walls,
  Unpeopled offices, untrodden stones?   70
And what hear there for welcome but my groans?
Therefore commend me; let him not come there
  o seek out sorrow that dwells everywhere.
  Desolate, desolate will I hence and die!
  he last leave of thee takes my weeping eye.   75

                                        Exeunt.

Scene III. [The lists at Coventry.]

Enter Lord Marshal and the Duke Aumerle.

Mar. My Lord Aumerle, is Harry Hereford armed?
Aum. Yea, at all points, and longs to enter in.
Mar. The Duke of Norfolk, sprightfully and bold,
Stays but the summons of the appellant's trumpet.
Aum. Why, then the champions are prepared, and   5
    stay
For nothing but His Majesty's approach.

The trumpets sound and the King enters with his
Nobles, Gaunt, Bushy, Bagot, Green, and others.
When they are set, enter Mowbray the Duke of Nor-
folk in arms, defendant, and Herald.

20. **God defend:** God forbid.
22. **issue:** children; heirs.
27. **truly:** in the name of truth; righteously.
32. **Depose him:** take his sworn statement.

King. Marshal, demand of yonder champion
The cause of his arrival here in arms.
Ask him his name and orderly proceed   10
To swear him in the justice of his cause.
   Mar. In God's name and the King's, say who thou art,
And why thou comest thus knightly clad in arms;
Against what man thou comest, and what thy quarrel.
Speak truly on thy knighthood and thy oath,   15
As so defend thee heaven and thy valor!
   Mowb. My name is Thomas Mowbray, Duke of
        Norfolk,
Who hither come engaged by my oath
(Which God defend a knight should violate!)   20
Both to defend my loyalty and truth
To God, my king, and his succeeding issue
Against the Duke of Hereford that appeals me;
And, by the grace of God and this mine arm,
To prove him, in defending of myself,   25
A traitor to my God, my king, and me;
And as I truly fight, defend me heaven!

The trumpets sound. Enter [Bolingbroke], Duke of
   Hereford, appellant, in armor, [and Herald].

   King. Marshal, ask yonder knight in arms
Both who he is and why he cometh hither
Thus plated in habiliments of war;   30
And formally, according to our law,
Depose him in the justice of his cause.

48. fair designs: just proceedings.

Mar. What is thy name? and wherefore comest
   thou hither,
Before King Richard in his royal lists?   35
Against whom comest thou? and what's thy quarrel?
Speak like a true knight, so defend thee heaven!
   Boling. Harry of Hereford, Lancaster, and Derby
Am I, who ready here do stand in arms
To prove, by God's grace and my body's valor   40
In lists on Thomas Mowbray, Duke of Norfolk,
That he is a traitor, foul and dangerous,
To God of heaven, King Richard, and to me;
And as I truly fight, defend me heaven!
   Mar. On pain of death, no person be so bold   45
Or daring-hardy as to touch the lists,
Except the Marshal and such officers
Appointed to direct these fair designs.
   Boling. Lord Marshal, let me kiss my sovereign's
   hand   50
And bow my knee before His Majesty;
For Mowbray and myself are like two men
That vow a long and weary pilgrimage.
Then let us take a ceremonious leave
And loving farewell of our several friends.   55
   Mar. The appellant in all duty greets your High-
   ness,
And craves to kiss your hand and take his leave.
   King. We will descend and fold him in our arms.
Cousin of Hereford, as thy cause is right,   60
So be thy fortune in this royal fight!

72. **regreet:** salute.

75. **regenerate:** reborn.

78. **proof:** additional strength. Proof armor was designed to resist penetration.

80. **waxen:** i.e., soft, as though made of wax.

81. **furbish:** brighten; glorify.

87. **amazing:** stunning; paralyzing; **casque:** helmet.

90. **to thrive:** aid me to thrive.

Farewell, my blood; which if today thou shed,
Lament we may, but not revenge thee dead.
    Boling. O, let no noble eye profane a tear
For me, if I be gored with Mowbray's spear.   65
As confident as is the falcon's flight
Against a bird do I with Mowbray fight.
My loving lord, I take my leave of you;
Of you, my noble cousin, Lord Aumerle;
Not sick, although I have to do with death,   70
But lusty, young, and cheerly drawing breath.
Lo, as at English feasts, so I regreet
The daintiest last, to make the end most sweet.
O thou, the earthly author of my blood,
Whose youthful spirit, in me regenerat   75
Doth with a twofold vigor lift me up
To reach at victory above my head,
Add proof unto mine armor with thy prayers,
And with thy blessings steel my lance's point,
That it may enter Mowbray's waxen coat   80
And furbish new the name of John o' Gaunt
Even in the lusty havior of his son.
    Gaunt. God in thy good cause make thee pros-
        perous!
Be swift like lightning in the execution,   85
And let thy blows, doubly redoubled,
Fall like amazing thunder on the casque
Of thy adverse pernicious enemy.
Rouse up thy youthful blood; be valiant and live.
    Boling. Mine innocence and St. George to thrive!   90
    Mowb. However God or fortune cast my lot,

101. **gentle:** quietly.
120. **approve:** prove.

There lives or dies, true to King Richard's throne,
A loyal, just, and upright gentleman.
Never did captive with a freer heart
Cast off his chains of bondage and embrace   95
His golden uncontrolled enfranchisement,
More than my dancing soul doth celebrate
This feast of battle with mine adversary.
Most mighty liege, and my companion peers,
Take from my mouth the wish of happy years.   100
As gentle and as jocund as to jest
Go I to fight. Truth hath a quiet breast.
    King. Farewell, my lord. Securely I espy
Virtue with valor couched in thine eye.
Order the trial, Marshal, and begin.   105
    Mar. Harry of Hereford, Lancaster, and Derby,
Receive thy lance, and God defend the right!
    Boling. Strong as a tower in hope, I cry amen.
    Mar. [*To an Officer*] Go bear this lance to Thomas,
        Duke of Norfolk.   110
    1. Herald. Harry of Hereford, Lancaster, and Derby
Stands here for God, his sovereign, and himself,
On pain to be found false and recreant,
To prove the Duke of Norfolk, Thomas Mowbray,
A traitor to his God, his king, and him,   115
And dares him to set forward to the fight.
    2. Herald. Here standeth Thomas Mowbray, Duke
        of Norfolk,
On pain to be found false and recreant,
Both to defend himself and to approve   120
Henry of Hereford, Lancaster, and Derby

126. **warder:** baton; a signal to stop the combat.
131. **While:** until; **return:** inform.
134. **For:** in order.
136. **for:** because.

To God, his sovereign, and to him disloyal,
Courageously and with a free desire
Attending but the signal to begin.
    Mar. Sound trumpets, and set forward combatants. 125
                      A charge sounded.
Stay! The King hath thrown his warder down.
    King. Let them lay by their helmets and their
        spears
And both return back to their chairs again.
Withdraw with us; and let the trumpets sound   130
While we return these dukes what we decree.
                      A long flourish.
Draw near,
And list what with our Council we have done.
For that our kingdom's earth should not be soiled
With that dear blood which it hath fostered;   135
And for our eyes do hate the dire aspect
Of civil wounds plowed up with neighbor's sword;
And for we think the eagle-winged pride
Of sky-aspiring and ambitious thoughts
With rival-hating envy set on you   140
To wake our peace, which in our country's cradle
Draws the sweet infant breath of gentle sleep;
Which so roused up with boist'rous untuned drums,
With harsh-resounding trumpets' dreadful bray
And grating shock of wrathful iron arms,   145
Might from our quiet confines fright fair peace
And make us wade even in our kindred's blood:
Therefore we banish you our territories.
You, cousin Hereford, upon pain of life,

161. **dateless:** endless; **dear:** bitter.
166. **dearer merit:** worthier reward.
173. **cunning:** cleverly fashioned.

Till twice five summers have enriched our fields   150
Shall not regreet our fair dominions
But tread the stranger paths of banishment.
    Boling. Your will be done. This must my comfort
    be:
That sun that warms you here shall shine on me,   155
And those his golden beams to you here lent
Shall point on me and gild my banishment.
    King. Norfolk, for thee remains a heavier doom,
Which I with some unwillingness pronounce:
The sly-slow hours shall not determinate   160
The dateless limit of thy dear exile.
The hopeless word of "never to return"
Breathe I against thee, upon pain of life.
    Mowb. A heavy sentence, my most sovereign liege,
And all unlooked for from your Highness' mouth.   165
A dearer merit, not so deep a maim
As to be cast forth in the common air,
Have I deserved at your Highness' hands.
The language I have learnt these forty years,
My native English, now I must forgo;   170
And now my tongue's use is to me no more
Than an unstringed viol or a harp,
Or like a cunning instrument cased up
Or, being open, put into his hands
That knows no touch to tune the harmony.   175
Within my mouth you have enjailed my tongue,
Doubly portcullised with my teeth and lips;
And dull, unfeeling, barren ignorance
Is made my jailer to attend on me.

181. **to be a pupil:** i.e., to learn a new language.

183. **breathing:** speaking; **breath:** words.

184. **boots:** profits; **be compassionate:** seek compassion.

185. **plaining:** lamenting.

189. **sword:** used for the swearing of oaths because the hilt formed a cross.

191. **part:** share in the allegiance owed to God.

198. **advised purpose:** deliberate appointment.

203. **so far as to mine enemy:** so far as I can speak to an enemy, this is my advice.

I am too old to fawn upon a nurse,   180
Too far in years to be a pupil now.
What is thy sentence then but speechless death,
Which robs my tongue from breathing native breath?
   King. It boots thee not to be compassionate.
After our sentence plaining comes too late.   185
   Mowb. Then thus I turn me from my country's light
To dwell in solemn shades of endless night.
   King. Return again and take an oath with thee.
Lay on our royal sword your banished hands;
Swear by the duty that you owe to God   190
(Our part therein we banish with yourselves)
To keep the oath that we administer:
You never shall, so help you truth and God,
Embrace each other's love in banishment;
Nor never look upon each other's face;   195
Nor never write, regreet, nor reconcile
This low'ring tempest of your homebred hate;
Nor never by advised purpose meet
To plot, contrive, or complot any ill
'Gainst us, our state, our subjects, or our land.   200
   Boling. I swear.
   Mowb. And I, to keep all this.
   Boling. Norfolk, so far as to mine enemy:
By this time, had the King permitted us,
One of our souls had wand'red in the air,   205
Banished this frail sepulcher of our flesh,
As now our flesh is banished from this land.
Confess thy treasons ere thou fly the realm.

216. **stray:** take the wrong path.
218. **glasses:** mirrors. His tears reflect his sorrow.
233. **extinct with:** extinguished by.
238. **sullen:** dismal.

Since thou hast far to go, bear not along
The clogging burden of a guilty soul.   210
    Mowb. No, Bolingbroke. If ever I were traitor,
My name be blotted from the book of life
And I from heaven banished as from hence!
But what thou art, God, thou, and I do know;
And all too soon, I fear, the King shall rue.   215
Farewell, my liege. Now no way can I stray.
Save back to England, all the world's my way.   *Exit.*
    King. Uncle, even in the glasses of thine eyes
I see thy grieved heart. Thy sad aspect
Hath from the number of his banished years   220
Plucked four away. [*To Bolingbroke*] Six frozen win-
        ters spent,
Return with welcome home from banishment.
    Boling. How long a time lies in one little word!
Four lagging winters and four wanton springs   225
End in a word, such is the breath of kings.
    Gaunt. I thank my liege that in regard of me
He shortens four years of my son's exile.
But little vantage shall I reap thereby;
For ere the six years that he hath to spend   230
Can change their moons and bring their times about,
My oil-dried lamp and time-bewasted light
Shall be extinct with age and endless night;
My inch of taper will be burnt and done,
And blindfold death not let me see my son.   235
    King. Why, uncle, thou hast many years to live.
    Gaunt. But not a minute, king, that thou canst give.
Shorten my days thou canst with sullen sorrow

v

241. **stop no wrinkle in his pilgrimage:** prevent the forming of not one wrinkle in the course of time.

242. **Thy word is current with him for my death:** i.e., as king, you have power to take my life.

244. **upon good advice:** as the result of careful deliberation.

245. **Whereto thy tongue a party verdict gave:** to which decision you gave assent.

252. **smooth:** gloss over.

253. **partial slander:** charge of partiality.

255. **looked when:** expected that.

And pluck nights from me, but not lend a morrow.
Thou canst help time to furrow me with age,   240
But stop no wrinkle in his pilgrimage.
Thy word is current with him for my death,
But dead, thy kingdom cannot buy my breath.
  King. Thy son is banished upon good advice,
Whereto thy tongue a party verdict gave.   245
Why at our justice seemst thou then to lour?
  Gaunt. Things sweet to taste prove in digestion
      sour.
You urged me as a judge; but I had rather
You would have bid me argue like a father.   250
O, had it been a stranger, not my child,
To smooth his fault I should have been more mild.
A partial slander sought I to avoid,
And in the sentence my own life destroyed.
Alas, I looked when some of you should say   255
I was too strict to make mine own away;
But you gave leave to my unwilling tongue
Against my will to do myself this wrong.
  King. Cousin, farewell; and, uncle, bid him so.
Six years we banish him, and he shall go.   260
                Flourish. Exit [*King with his Train*].
  Aum. Cousin, farewell. What presence must not
      know,
From where you do remain let paper show.
  Mar. My lord, no leave take I; for I will ride,
As far as land will let me, by your side.   265
  Gaunt. O, to what purpose dost thou hoard thy
      words

283. **remember:** remind.

285–88. **Must I not serve a long apprentice-hood/To foreign passages and, in the end,/Having my freedom, boast of nothing else/But that I was a journeyman to grief:** having served an apprenticeship in foreign ways, I will find myself trained only in grief. The usual term of apprenticeship was seven years, at the end of which time the apprentice became a journeyman.

289–90. **All places that the eye of heaven visits/Are to a wise man ports and happy havens:** proverbial: A valiant (wise) man esteemeth every place to be his own country.

296. **purchase:** acquire.

That thou returnest no greeting to thy friends?
   Boling. I have too few to take my leave of you,
When the tongue's office should be prodigal   270
To breathe the abundant dolor of the heart.
   Gaunt. Thy grief is but thy absence for a time.
   Boling. Joy absent, grief is present for that time.
   Gaunt. What is six winters? They are quickly gone.
   Boling. To men in joy; but grief makes one hour ten. 275
   Gaunt. Call it a travel that thou takest for pleasure.
   Boling. My heart will sigh when I miscall it so,
Which finds it an enforced pilgrimage.
   Gaunt. The sullen passage of thy weary steps
Esteem as foil wherein thou are to set   280
The precious jewel of thy home return.
   Boling. Nay, rather every tedious stride I make
Will but remember me what a deal of world
I wander from the jewels that I love.
Must I not serve a long apprenticehood   285
To foreign passages and, in the end,
Having my freedom, boast of nothing else
But that I was a journeyman to grief?
   Gaunt. All places that the eye of heaven visits
Are to a wise man ports and happy havens.   290
Teach thy necessity to reason thus;
There is no virtue like necessity.
Think not the King did banish thee,
But thou the King. Woe doth the heavier sit
Where it perceives it is but faintly borne.   295
Go, say I sent thee forth to purchase honor,
And not, the King exiled thee; or suppose

303. **presence strowed:** royal presence chamber strewn with rushes.

306. **gnarling:** snarling.

307. **sets:** holds.

313. **fantastic:** fancied; imagined.

318. **bring:** escort.

Devouring pestilence hangs in our air
And thou art flying to a fresher clime.
Look what thy soul holds dear, imagine it   300
To lie that way thou goest, not whence thou comest.
Suppose the singing birds musicians,
The grass whereon thou treadest the presence stowed,
The flowers fair ladies, and thy steps no more
Than a delightful measure or a dance;   305
For gnarling sorrow hath less power to bite
The man that mocks at it and sets it light.
   Boling. O, who can hold a fire in his hand
By thinking on the frosty caucasus,
Or cloy the hungry edge of appetite   310
By bare imagination of a feast?
Or wallow naked in December snow
By thinking on fantastic summer's heat?
O, no! The apprehension of the good
Gives but the greater feeling to the worse.   315
Fell sorrow's tooth doth never rankle more
Than when he bites but lanceth not the sore.
   Gaunt. Come, come, my son, I'll bring thee on thy
     way.
Had I thy youth and cause, I would not stay.   320
   Boling. Then, England's ground, farewell; sweet
     soil, adieu,
My mother, and my nurse, that bears me yet!
Where'er I wander, boast of this I can,
Though banished, yet a trueborn Englishman.   325
                     Exeunt.

I. iv. Hereford's departure is described to the King, who feels obvious relief at having him out of the way. Unrest in Ireland now demands attention and the King consults with his favorites about raising funds to finance an expedition. When word comes that old Gaunt is seriously ill, the King greedily contemplates the appropriation of Gaunt's wealth and movables in the event of his death.

‖‖‖‖‖‖‖‖‖‖‖‖‖‖‖‖‖‖‖‖‖‖‖‖‖‖‖

2. **high:** haughty.
7. **for me:** for my part.
10. **rheum:** moisture.

Scene IV. [London. The court.]

*Enter the King, with Green and Bagot, at one door,
and the Lord Aumerle at another.*

King. We did observe. Cousin Aumerle,
How far brought you high Hereford on his way?
   Aum. I brought high Hereford, if you call him so,
But to the next highway, and there I left him.
   King. And say, what store of parting tears were   5
   shed?
   Aum. Faith, none for me; except the northeast
   wind,
Which then blew bitterly against our faces,
Awaked the sleeping rheum, and so by chance   10
Did grace our hollow parting with a tear.
   King. What said our cousin when you parted with
   him?
   Aum. "Farewell!"
And, for my heart disdained that my tongue   15
Should so profane the word, that taught me craft
To counterfeit oppression of such grief
That words seemed buried in my sorrow's grave.
Marry, would the word "farewell" have length'ned
   hours   20
And added years to his short banishment,
He should have had a volume of farewells;
But since it would not, he had none of me.
   King. He is our cousin, cousin; but 'tis doubt,

33. **underbearing:** forbearance.

34. **affects:** affections; i.e., carry their affections with him into banishment.

39. **in reversion his:** legally due him on the death of the present owner.

44. **Expedient manage:** speedy arrangement.

50. **farm our royal realm:** borrow money against the revenues due the Crown.

53. **blank charters:** documents promising money with the amounts left blank.

When time shall call him home from banishment,   25
Whether our kinsman come to see his friends.
Ourself and Bushy, Bagot here, and Green
Observed his courtship to the common people;
How he did seem to dive into their hearts
With humble and familiar courtesy;   30
What reverence he did throw away on slaves,
Wooing poor craftsmen with the craft of smiles
And patient underbearing of his fortune,
As 'twere to banish their affects with him.
Off goes his bonnet to an oyster wench;   35
A brace of draymen bid God speed him well
And had the tribute of his supple knee,
With "Thanks, my countrymen, my loving friends";
As were our England in reversion his,
And he our subjects' next degree in hope.   40
   Green. Well, he is gone, and with him go these
      thoughts!
Now for the rebels which stand out in Ireland,
Expedient manage must be made, my liege,
Ere further leisure yield them further means   45
For their advantage and your Highness' loss.
   King. We will ourself in person to this war;
And, for our coffers, with too great a court
And liberal largess, are grown somewhat light,
We are enforced to farm our royal realm,   50
The revenue whereof shall furnish us
For our affairs in hand. If that come short,
Our substitutes at home shall have blank charters,
Whereto, when they shall know what men are rich,

57. presently: at once.

They shall subscribe them for large sums of gold   55
And send them after to supply our wants,
For we will make for Ireland presently.

Enter Bushy.

Bushy, what news?
 Bushy. Old John of Gaunt is grievous sick, my lord,
Suddenly taken, and hath sent posthaste   60
To entreat your Majesty to visit him.
 King. Where lies he?
 Bushy. At Ely House.
 King. Now put it, God, in the physician's mind
To help him to his grave immediately!   65
The lining of his coffers shall make coats
To deck our soldiers for these Irish wars.
Come, gentlemen, let's all go visit him.
Pray God we may make haste, and come too late!
 All. Amen.   70

           Exeunt.

THE TRAGEDY OF

RICHARD
THE SECOND

ACT II

II. i. King Richard visits Gaunt's sickbed. The dying man reproaches him bitterly for his mismanagement of the country's affairs and prophesies that his wasteful conduct will shortly bring about his own destruction. When Gaunt has breathed his last the King immediately orders the seizure of all his movable property. In vain Gaunt's brother York urges the King to honor his promise to Gaunt's son, Hereford, that he will be allowed to lay claim to his Lancaster properties. The King departs, planning to sail for Ireland the following day; he leaves the kingdom in York's charge.

‖‖‖‖‖‖‖‖‖‖‖‖‖‖‖‖‖‖‖‖‖‖‖‖‖

14. **glose:** utter pleasant or flattering speeches.
17. **is sweetest last:** outlasts all other sweet things.

ACT II

Scene I. [London. Ely House.]

Enter John of Gaunt, sick, with the Duke of York, etc.

Gaunt. Will the King come, that I may breathe my
    last
In wholesome counsel to his unstaid youth?
    York. Vex not yourself nor strive not with your
    breath,   5
For all in vain comes counsel to his ear.
    Gaunt. O, but they say the tongues of dying men
Enforce attention like deep harmony.
Where words are scarce, they are seldom spent in
    vain,   10
For they breathe truth that breathe their words in
    pain.
He that no more must say is listened more
Than they whom youth and ease have taught to glose.
More are men's ends marked than their lives before. 15
The setting sun, and music at the close,
As the last taste of sweets, is sweetest last,
Writ in remembrance more than things long past.

19. **my live's counsel:** my counsel while I lived.

20. **death's sad tale:** solemn dying words.

22. **fond:** J. P. Collier's correction of the Quarto, which reads "found"; **the wise are fond:** i.e., even the wise foolishly value.

23. **venom:** venomous; the use of a noun for an adjective was common in Elizabethan usage.

25. **proud:** splendid in attire.

26. **tardy-apish:** belatedly imitative; i.e., given to imitation of fashions no longer new.

29. **there's no respect how vile:** no consideration is given to its vileness.

32. **will doth mutiny with wit's regard:** unconsidered desire rebels against wise judgment.

34. **that breath wilt thou lose:** i.e., your words will be uttered in vain.

40. **betimes . . . betimes:** quickly . . . early in the day.

45. **earth of majesty:** world of majestic grandeur.

46. **demiparadise:** near unto paradise.

Though Richard my live's counsel would not hear,
My death's sad tale may yet undeaf his ear.   20
  York. No; it is stopped with other flattering sounds,
As praises, of whose taste the wise are fond,
Lascivious meters, to whose venom sound
The open ear of youth doth always listen;
Report of fashions in proud Italy,   25
Whose manners still our tardy-apish nation
Limps after in base imitation.
Where doth the world thrust forth a vanity
(So it be new, there's no respect how vile)
That is not quickly buzzed into his ears?   30
Then all too late comes counsel to be heard
Where will doth mutiny with wit's regard.
Direct not him whose way himself will choose.
'Tis breath thou lackst, and that breath wilt thou lose.
  Gaunt. Methinks I am a prophet new inspired   35
And thus, expiring, do foretell of him:
His rash fierce blaze of riot cannot last,
For violent fires soon burn out themselves;
Small show'rs last long, but sudden storms are short;
He tires betimes that spurs too fast betimes;   40
With eager feeding food doth choke the feeder;
Light vanity, insatiate cormorant,
Consuming means, soon preys upon itself.
This royal throne of kings, this scept'red isle,
This earth of majesty, this seat of Mars,   45
This other Eden, demiparadise,
This fortress built by Nature for herself
Against infection and the hand of war,

53. **envy:** malice.

56. **by:** because of.

64. **tenement:** land or residence rented from another; **pelting:** paltry.

66. **envious:** malevolent.

68. **inky blots and rotten parchment bonds:** i.e., the documents certifying the lease of the royal revenues.

74. **raged:** aphetic form of "enraged."

This happy breed of men, this little world,
This precious stone set in the silver sea,   50
Which serves it in the office of a wall,
Or as a moat defensive to a house,
Against the envy of less happier lands;
This blessed plot, this earth, this realm, this England,
This nurse, this teeming womb of royal kings,   55
Feared by their breed and famous by their birth,
Renowned for their deeds as far from home,
For Christian service and true chivalry,
As is the sepulcher in stubborn Jewry
Of the world's ransom, blessed Mary's son;   60
This land of such dear souls, this dear dear land,
Dear for her reputation through the world,
Is now leased out (I die pronouncing it)
Like to a tenement or pelting farm.
England, bound in with the triumphant sea,   65
Whose rocky shore beats back the envious siege
Of wat'ry Neptune, is now bound in with shame,
With inky blots and rotten parchment bonds.
That England that was wont to conquer others
Hath made a shameful conquest of itself.   70
Ah, would the scandal vanish with my life,
How happy then were my ensuing death!

Enter King, Queen, Aumerle, Bushy, Green, Bagot,
Ross, and Willoughby.

York. The King is come. Deal mildly with his youth;
For young hot colts, being raged, do rage the more.

78. **composition:** physical condition.

82. **watched:** spent sleepless nights; kept vigil.

88. **inherits:** possesses.

89. **nicely:** ingeniously and frivolously.

90. **to mock:** in mocking.

91. **kill my name in me:** i.e., cause the name and fame of his family to die with him, since his heir has been banished from the realm.

99. **Ill in myself to see, and in thee seeing ill:** i.e., unable to see well, yet seeing evil in you.

Queen. How fares our noble uncle Lancaster? 75
King. What comfort, man? How is't with aged
  Gaunt?
Gaunt. O, how that name befits my composition!
Old Gaunt indeed, and gaunt in being old.
Within me grief hath kept a tedious fast; 80
And who abstains from meat that is not gaunt?
For sleeping England long time have I watched;
Watching breeds leanness, leanness is all gaunt.
The pleasure that some fathers feed upon
Is my strict fast—I mean my children's looks— 85
And therein fasting hast thou made me gaunt.
Gaunt am I for the grave, gaunt as a grave,
Whose hollow womb inherits naught but bones.
  King. Can sick men play so nicely with their names?
  Gaunt. No, misery makes sport to mock itself. 90
Since thou dost seek to kill my name in me,
I mock my name, great king, to flatter thee.
  King. Should dying men flatter with those that live?
  Gaunt. No, no! men living flatter those that die.
  King. Thou, now a-dying, sayst thou flatterest me. 95
  Gaunt. O, no! thou diest, though I the sicker be.
  King. I am in health, I breathe, and see thee ill.
  Gaunt. Now, He that made me knows I see thee ill;
Ill in myself to see, and in thee seeing ill.
Thy deathbed is no lesser than thy land, 100
Wherein thou liest in reputation sick;
And thou, too careless patient as thou art,
Committst thy anointed body to the cure
Of those physicians that first wounded thee.

105. **sit within thy crown:** influence your royal will.

119. **Thy state of law is bondslave to the law:** i.e., you are as subject to the laws governing property as any other landlord.

125. **his:** its.

128. **roundly:** bluntly.

132. **the pelican:** ancient natural history described the pelican as nourishing its young with its own flesh and blood.

133. **caroused:** swilled.

The pelican feeding its young.
From *An Early English Version of Hortus Sanitatis* (1941).

A thousand flatterers sit within thy crown,   105
Whose compass is no bigger than thy head;
And yet, encaged in so small a verge,
The waste is no whit lesser than thy land.
O, had thy grandsire, with a prophet's eye,
Seen how his son's son should destroy his sons,   110
From forth thy reach he would have laid thy shame,
Deposing thee before thou wert possessed,
Which art possessed now to depose thyself.
Why, cousin, wert thou regent of the world,
It were a shame to let this land by lease;   115
But, for thy world enjoying but this land,
Is it not more than shame to shame it so?
Landlord of England art thou now, not King.
Thy state of law is bondslave to the law,
And thou—   120
     King.   A lunatic lean-witted fool,
Presuming on an ague's privilege,
Darest with thy frozen admonition
Make pale our cheek, chasing the royal blood
With fury from his native residence,   125
Now, by my seat's right royal majesty,
Wert thou not brother to great Edward's son,
This tongue that runs so roundly in thy head
Should run thy head from thy unreverent shoulders.
     Gaunt. O, spare me not, my brother Edward's son,   130
For that I was his father Edward's son!
That blood already, like the pelican,
Hast thou tapped out and drunkenly caroused.
My brother Gloucester, plain well-meaning soul

145. **sullens:** sulks.

151. **As Hereford's love, so his:** i.e., he loves me as much as Hereford does—little.

159. **bankrout:** bankrupt.

Edward III.
John Taylor, *All the Works* (1630).

(Whom fair befall in heaven 'mongst happy souls!),   135
May be a precedent and witness good
That thou respectst not spilling Edward's blood.
Join with the present sickness that I have,
And thy unkindness be like crooked age,
To crop at once a too long withered flower.   140
Live in thy shame, but die not shame with thee!
These words hereafter thy tormentors be!
Convey me to my bed, then to my grave.
Love they to live that love and honor have.
                    Exit [borne off by Attendants].
    King. And let them die that age and sullens have;   145
For both hast thou, and both become the grave.
    York. I do beseech your Majesty impute his words
To wayward sickliness and age in him.
He loves you, on my life, and holds you dear
As Harry Duke of Hereford, were he here.   150
    King. Right, you say true! As Hereford's love, so his;
As theirs, so mine; and all be as it is!

            Enter Northumberland.

    North. My liege, old Gaunt commends him to your
        Majesty.
    King. What says he?   155
    North.   Nay, nothing; all is said.
His tongue is now a stringless instrument;
Words, life, and all, old Lancaster hath spent.
    York. Be York the next that must be bankrout so!
Though death be poor, it ends a mortal woe.   160

162. **must be:** is yet to come. The course of man's life on earth was often likened to a pilgrimage.

164. **rugheaded:** shaggy-haired; **kerns:** Irish foot soldiers, who acted as freebooters rather than as disciplined troops.

165. **no venom else:** no venomous snake, referring to St. Patrick's expulsion of snakes from Ireland.

175–76. **the prevention of poor Bolingbroke/About his marriage:** according to Holinshed, the King accused Bolingbroke of treason and urged the King of France to prevent Bolingbroke's projected marriage with the daughter of the Duke of Berry.

178. **wrinkle:** frown.

185. **Accomplished with the number of thy hours:** i.e., at your age.

A rugheaded kern.
From John Derricke, *The Image of Ireland* (1581; 1883).

King. The ripest fruit first falls, and so doth he;
His time is spent, our pilgrimage must be.
So much for that. Now for our Irish wars.
We must supplant those rough rugheaded kerns,
Which live like venom where no venom else   165
But only they have privilege to live.
And, for these great affairs do ask some charge,
Toward our assistance we do seize to us
The plate, coin, revenues, and movables
Whereof our uncle Gaunt did stand possessed.   170

York. How long shall I be patient? Ah, how long
Shall tender duty make me suffer wrong?
Not Gloucester's death, nor Hereford's banishment,
Nor Gaunt's rebukes, nor England's private wrongs,
Nor the prevention of poor Bolingbroke   175
About his marriage, nor my own disgrace,
Have ever made me sour my patient cheek
Or bend one wrinkle on my sovereign's face.
I am the last of noble Edward's sons,
Of whom thy father, Prince of Wales, was first.   180
In war was never lion raged more fierce,
In peace was never gentle lamb more mild,
Than was that young and princely gentleman.
His face thou hast, for even so looked he
Accomplished with the number of thy hours;   185
But when he frowned, it was against the French
And not against his friends. His noble hand
Did win what he did spend, and spent not that
Which his triumphant father's hand had won.
His hands were guilty of no kindred blood,   190

199. **royalties:** rights granted by the king to a subject, particularly those concerning revenue.

206. **ensue:** follow.

211. **letters patents:** royal concession. Although banished, Bolingbroke had been granted the right to have attorneys press his claim to his father's lands, which otherwise would revert to the Crown.

212–13. **sue/His livery:** sue for the delivery of his inheritance; **homage:** the homage that Bolingbroke would offer the King as part of the ritual of claiming his inheritance.

But bloody with the enemies of his kin.
O Richard! York is too far gone with grief,
Or else he never would compare between.
 King. Why, uncle, what's the matter?
 York.   O my liege, 195
Pardon me, if you please; if not, I, pleased
Not to be pardoned, am content withal.
Seek you to seize and gripe into your hands
The royalties and rights of banished Hereford?
Is not Gaunt dead? and doth not Hereford live? 200
Was not Gaunt just? and is not Harry true?
Did not the one deserve to have an heir?
Is not his heir a well-deserving son?
Take Hereford's rights away, and take from Time
His charters and his customary rights; 205
Let not tomorrow then ensue today;
Be not thyself—for how art thou a king
But by fair sequence and succession?
Now, afore God (God forbid I say true!),
If you do wrongfully seize Hereford's rights, 210
Call in the letters patents that he hath
By his attorneys general to sue
His livery, and deny his off'red homage,
You pluck a thousand dangers on your head,
You lose a thousand well-disposed hearts, 215
And prick my tender patience to those thoughts
Which honor and allegiance cannot think.
 King. Think what you will, we seize into our hands
His plate, his goods, his money, and his lands.
 York. I'll not be by the while. My liege, farewell. 220

222. **by:** concerning.
223. **events:** outcomes.
226. **see:** look after.
227. **trow:** think.
237. **great:** swollen with emotion.
239. **liberal:** free and frank.
243. **Tends that thou wouldst:** i.e., does the tenor of what you would say concern.

What will ensue hereof there's none can tell;
But by bad courses may be understood
That their events can never fall out good.   *Exit.*

 King. Go, Bushy, to the Earl of Wiltshire straight.
Bid him repair to us to Ely House   225
To see this business. Tomorrow next
We will for Ireland; and 'tis time, I trow.
And we create, in absence of ourself,
Our uncle York Lord Governor of England;
For he is just and always loved us well.   230
Come on, our queen. Tomorrow must we part.
Be merry, for our time of stay is short.

 Flourish. Exeunt. Manent Northumberland,
       Willoughby, and Ross.

 North. Well, lords, the Duke of Lancaster is dead.
 Ross. And living too; for now his son is Duke.
 Wil. Barely in title, not in revenues.   235
 North. Richly in both, if justice had her right.
 Ross. My heart is great; but it must break with
  silence,
Ere't be disburdened with a liberal tongue.
 North. Nay, speak thy mind; and let him ne'er 240
  speak more
That speaks thy words again to do thee harm!
 Wil. Tends that thou wouldst speak to the Duke of
  Hereford?
If it be so, out with it boldly, man!   245
Quick is mine ear to hear of good toward him.

252. **mo:** more.

259. **pilled:** pillaged; robbed.

264. **benevolences:** exactions of money with the pretense of their being free gifts; **wot:** know.

265. **a:** in.

269. **achieved:** won.

273. **Reproach and dissolution:** a shameful end.

275. **burthenous:** burdensome.

Ross. No good at all that I can do for him;
Unless you call it good to pity him,
Bereft and gelded of his patrimony.
   North. Now, afore God, 'tis shame such wrongs are 250
     borne
In him a royal prince and many mo
Of noble blood in this declining land.
The King is not himself, but basely led
By flatterers; and what they will inform,   255
Merely in hate, 'gainst any of us all,
That will the King severely prosecute
'Gainst us, our lives, our children, and our heirs.
   Ross. The commons hath he pilled with grievous
     taxes   260
And quite lost their hearts; the nobles hath he fined
For ancient quarrels and quite lost their hearts.
   Wil. And daily new exactions are devised,
As blanks, benevolences, and I wot not what;
But what, a God's name, doth become of this?   265
   North. Wars have not wasted it, for warred he
     hath not,
But basely yielded upon compromise
That which his noble ancestors achieved with blows.
More hath he spent in peace than they in wars.   270
   Ross. The Earl of Wiltshire hath the realm in farm.
   Wil. The King's grown bankrout, like a broken man.
   North. Reproach and dissolution hangeth over him.
   Ross. He hath not money for these Irish wars,
His burthenous taxations notwithstanding,   275
But by the robbing of the banished Duke.

280. **sore:** heavily.

281. **strike:** i.e., strike sail; **securely:** because of overconfidence.

283. **unavoided:** unavoidable.

295. **Brittaine:** Brittany.

296. **Cobham:** a line has dropped out at this point. It was the Earl of Arundel's son Thomas who escaped from the Duke of Exeter.

303. **tall:** splendid.

304. **expedience:** speed.

North. His noble kinsman. Most degenerate king!
But, lords, we hear this fearful tempest sing,
Yet seek no shelter to avoid the storm.
We see the wind sit sore upon our sails,   280
And yet we strike not but securely perish.
    Ross. We see the very wrack that we must suffer,
And unavoided is the danger now
For suffering so the causes of our wrack.
    North. Not so. Even through the hollow eyes of 285
        death
I spy life peering; but I dare not say
How near the tidings of our comfort is.
    Wil. Nay, let us share thy thoughts as thou dost
        ours.   290
    Ross. Be confident to speak, Northumberland.
We three are but thyself, and speaking so,
Thy words are but as thoughts. Therefore be bold.
    North. Then thus: I have from Le Port Blanc, a bay
In Brittaine, received intelligence   295
That Harry Duke of Hereford, Rainold Lord Cobham,
That late broke from the Duke of Exeter,
His brother, Archbishop late of Canterbury,
Sir Thomas Erpingham, Sir John Ramston,
Sir John Norbery, Sir Robert Waterton, and Francis 300
        Quoint,
All these well furnished by the Duke of Brittaine
With eight tall ships, three thousand men of war,
Are making hither with all due expedience
And shortly mean to touch our northern shore.   305

309. **Imp out:** strengthen by grafting on new feathers; a term from falconry.

313. **in post:** as fast as possible.

318. **Hold out:** i.e., if it holds out.

░░░

II. ii. Two of the King's favorites, Bushy and Bagot, try to console the Queen, who feels a foreboding sorrow out of proportion to the mere fact of her husband's absence. Her fears seem confirmed when Green reports that Bolingbroke has landed and that a number of lords, including Northumberland and his son, have joined him. York has further bad news: his hope of borrowing money from his sister-in-law, the Duchess of Gloucester, vanishes when he learns of her death; the King has alienated the commons; and York sees no way to finance the raising of troops to repel Bolingbroke. Bushy and Green depart for Bristol to join the Earl of Wiltshire, and Bagot heads for Ireland to join the King.

Perhaps they had ere this, but that they stay
The first departing of the King for Ireland.
If then we shall shake off our slavish yoke,
Imp out our drooping country's broken wing,
Redeem from broking pawn the blemished crown,   310
Wipe off the dust that hides our scepter's gilt,
And make high majesty look like itself,
Away with me in post to Ravenspurgh;
But if you faint, as fearing to do so,
Stay and be secret, and myself will go.   315

    Ross. To horse, to horse! Urge doubts to them that
      fear.

    Wil. Hold out my horse, and I will first be there.
                               Exeunt.

Scene II. [Windsor Castle.]

Enter the Queen, Bushy, Bagot.

Bushy. Madam, your Majesty is too much sad.
You promised, when you parted with the King,
To lay aside life-harming heaviness
And entertain a cheerful disposition.

    Queen. To please the King, I did; to please myself,   5
I cannot do it. Yet I know no cause
Why I should welcome such a guest as grief
Save bidding farewell to so sweet a guest
As my sweet Richard. Yet again, methinks,
Some unborn sorrow, ripe in Fortune's womb,   10

19. **perspectives:** Elizabethan toys that gave a distorted image from a certain angle.

23–5. **Find shapes of grief more than himself to wail,/Which, looked on as it is, is naught but shadows/Of what it is not:** i.e., see images of grief more distressing than your grief for your husband; these images rightly viewed are only shadows of true grief.

29. **for:** in place of.

33–4. **As, though on thinking on no thought I think,/Makes me with heavy nothing faint and shrink:** that though I try not to think of anything distressing, I am oppressed by a sorrow that has no basis in reality.

35. **conceit:** imagination.

36. **nothing less:** a contradiction of Bushy's words; **still:** always.

40. **'Tis in reversion that I do possess:** i.e., my grief is something that will be yielded to me in the future—like property inherited by me; see **reversion,** I. iv. 39.

Is coming towards me, and my inward soul
With nothing trembles. At something it grieves
More than with parting from my lord the King.

 Bushy. Each substance of a grief hath twenty
  shadows,   15
Which shows like grief itself but is not so;
For sorrow's eye, glazed with blinding tears,
Divides one thing entire to many objects,
Like perspectives, which rightly gazed upon,
Show nothing but confusion; eyed awry,   20
Distinguish form. So your sweet Majesty,
Looking awry upon your lord's departure,
Find shapes of grief more than himself to wail,
Which, looked on as it is, is naught but shadows
Of what it is not. Then, thrice-gracious Queen, 25
More than your lord's departure weep not. More's not
  seen;
Or if it be, 'tis with false sorrow's eye,
Which for things true weeps things imaginary.

 Queen. It may be so; but yet my inward soul 30
Persuades me it is otherwise. Howe'er it be,
I cannot but be sad—so heavy sad
As, though on thinking on no thought I think,
Makes me with heavy nothing faint and shrink.

 Bushy. 'Tis nothing but conceit, my gracious lady. 35

 Queen. 'Tis nothing less. Conceit is still derived
From some forefather grief. Mine is not so,
For nothing hath begot my something grief,
Or something hath the nothing that I grieve.
'Tis in reversion that I do possess;   40

47. **good hope:** favorable expectation.
53. **repeals:** recalls.
57. **that:** what.

But what it is that is not yet known what,
I cannot name. 'Tis nameless woe, I wot.

Enter Green.

   Green. God save your Majesty! and well met,
    gentlemen.
I hope the King is not yet shipped for Ireland.   45
   Queen. Why hopest thou so? 'Tis better hope he is;
For his designs crave haste, his haste good hope.
Then wherefore dost thou hope he is not shipped?
   Green. That he, our hope, might have retired his
    power   50
And driven into despair an enemy's hope
Who strongly hath set footing in this land.
The banished Bolingbroke repeals himself
And with uplifted arms is safe arrived
At Ravenspurgh.   55
   Queen.   Now God in heaven forbid!
   Green. Ah, madam, 'tis too true; and that is worse,
The Lord Northumberland, his son young Henry
    Percy,
The Lords of Ross, Beaumond, and Willoughby,   60
With all their powerful friends, are fled to him.
   Bushy. Why have you not proclaimed Northumber-
    land
And all the rest revolted faction traitors?
   Green. We have; whereupon the Earl of Worcester   65
Hath broken his staff, resigned his stewardship,

70. **dismal:** ill-omened; **heir:** offspring.
71. **prodigy:** monstrous birth.
77. **cozening:** cheating.
80. **lingers in extremity:** prolongs in the utmost agony.
82. **signs of war:** a gorget, a portion of armor worn about the neck.
83. **careful:** anxious.
92. **surfeit:** i.e., excesses of conduct.

And all the household servants fled with him to
    Bolingbroke.
  Queen. So, Green, thou art the midwife to my woe,
And Bolingbroke my sorrow's dismal heir.   70
Now hath my soul brought forth her prodigy;
And I, a gasping new-delivered mother,
Have woe to woe, sorrow to sorrow joined.
  Bushy. Despair not, madam.
  Queen.   Who shall hinder me?   75
I will despair, and be at enmity
With cozening Hope. He is a flatterer,
A parasite, a keeper-back of Death,
Who gently would dissolve the bands of life,
Which false hope lingers in extremity.   80

Enter York.

  Green. Here comes the Duke of York.
  Queen. With signs of war about his aged neck.
O, full of careful business are his looks!
Uncle, for God's sake, speak comfortable words!
  York. Should I do so, I should belie my thoughts.   85
Comfort's in heaven, and we are on the earth,
Where nothing lives but crosses, cares, and grief.
Your husband, he is gone to save far off,
Whilst others come to make him lose at home.
Here am I left to underprop his land,   90
Who, weak with age, cannot support myself.
Now comes the sick hour that his surfeit made;
Now shall he try his friends that flattered him.

106. **God for his mercy:** God have mercy on us.
109. **untruth:** infidelity.

Enter a Servant.

Serv. My lord, your son was gone before I came.

York. He was? Why, so! Go all which way it will!   95
The nobles they are fled, the commons they are cold
And will, I fear, revolt on Hereford's side.
Sirrah, get thee to Plashy to my sister Gloucester;
Bid her send me presently a thousand pound.
Hold, take my ring.   100

Serv. My lord, I had forgot to tell your lordship
Today, as I came by, I called there—
But I shall grieve you to report the rest.

York. What is't, knave?

Serv. An hour before I came the Duchess died.   105

York. God for his mercy! what a tide of woes
Comes rushing on this woeful land at once!
I know not what to do. I would to God
(So my untruth had not provoked him to it)
The King had cut off my head with my brother's.   110
What, are there no posts dispatched for Ireland?
How shall we do for money for these wars?
Come, sister—cousin, I would say; pray pardon me.—
Go, fellow, get thee home, provide some carts
And bring away the armor that is there.   115

                              [*Exit Servant.*]

Gentlemen, will you go muster men? If I
Know how or which way to order these affairs,
Thus thrust disorderly into my hands,
Never believe me. Both are my kinsmen.

124. **somewhat:** something.
127. **presently:** immediately.

The one is my sovereign, whom both my oath   120
And duty bids defend; t'other again
Is my kinsman, whom the King hath wronged,
Whom conscience and my kindred bids to right.
Well, somewhat we must do. Come, cousin, I'll
Dispose of you.   125
Gentlemen, go muster up your men,
And meet me presently at Berkeley Castle.
I should to Plashy too,
But time will not permit. All is uneven,
And everything is left at six and seven.   130

                    Exeunt Duke, Queen.

Bushy. The wind sits fair for news to go for Ireland,
But none returns. For us to levy power
Proportionable to the enemy
Is all unpossible.

Green. Besides, our nearness to the King in love   135
Is near the hate of those love not the King.

Bagot. And that's the wavering commons; for their
  love
Lies in their purses, and whoso empties them,
By so much fills their hearts with deadly hate.   140

Bushy. Wherein the King stands generally condemned.

Bagot. If judgment lie in them, then so do we,
Because we ever have been near the King.

Green. Well, I will for refuge straight to Bristow   145
  Castle.
The Earl of Wiltshire is already there.

148. **office:** service.

||||||||||||||||||||||||||||||||||||||||||||||||||||||

II. iii. Bolingbroke and Northumberland, riding
for Bristol, are joined by Northumberland's son,
Henry Percy, Ross, and Willoughby. York meets
them near Berkeley Castle and charges Bolingbroke
with treason, but is assured by both that all Bolingbroke seeks is his rightful inheritance. York declares
himself neutral but invites them to spend the night
with him at the castle.

Bushy. Thither will I with you; for little office
The hateful commons will perform for us,
Except like curs to tear us all to pieces.   150
Will you go along with us?

Bagot. No; I will to Ireland to His Majesty.
Farewell. If heart's presages be not vain,
We three here part that ne'er shall meet again.

Bushy. That's as York thrives to beat back Boling- 155
    broke.

Green. Alas, poor Duke! The task he undertakes
Is numb'ring sands and drinking oceans dry.
Where one on his side fights, thousands will fly.

Bagot. Farewell at once—for once, for all, and ever. 160

Bushy. Well, we may meet again.

Bagot.   I fear me, never.

                                    Exeunt.

Scene III. [The wilds in Gloucestershire.]

Enter [Bolingbroke] the Duke of Hereford,
    and Northumberland.

Boling. How far is it, my lord, to Berkeley now?

North. Believe me, noble lord,
I am a stranger here in Gloucestershire.
These high wild hills and rough uneven ways
Draws out our miles and makes them wearisome;   5
And yet your fair discourse hath been as sugar,

9. **Cotshall:** probably Shakespeare's pronunciation of Cotswold.

12. **tediousness and process:** tedious course.

Making the hard way sweet and delectable.
But I bethink me what a weary way
From Ravenspurgh to Cotshall will be found
In Ross and Willoughby, wanting your company,   10
Which, I protest, hath very much beguiled
The tediousness and process of my travel;
But theirs is sweet'ned with the hope to have
The present benefit which I possess;
And hope to joy is little less in joy   15
Than hope enjoyed. By this the weary lords
Shall make their way seem short, as mine hath done
By sight of what I have, your noble company.
    Boling. Of much less value is my company
Than your good words. But who comes here?   20

Enter Harry Percy.

    North. It is my son, young Harry Percy,
Sent from my brother Worcester, whencesoever.
Harry, how fares your uncle?
    Percy. I had thought, my lord, to have learned his
        health of you.   25
    North. Why, is he not with the Queen?
    Percy. No, my good lord; he hath forsook the court,
Broken his staff of office, and dispersed
The household of the King.
    North.   What was his reason?   30
He was not so resolved when last we spake together.

45. **tender:** offer.
48. **approved:** proved.
53. **still:** always.
61. **estimate:** reputation.

Percy. Because your lordship was proclaimed
   traitor.
But he, my lord, is gone to Ravenspurgh
To offer service to the Duke of Hereford;   35
And sent me over by Berkeley to discover
What power the Duke of York had levied there;
Then with directions to repair to Ravenspurgh.
   North. Have you forgot the Duke of Hereford, boy?
   Percy. No, my good lord, for that is not forgot   40
Which ne'er I did remember. To my knowledge,
I never in my life did look on him.
   North. Then learn to know him now. This is the
   Duke.
   Percy. My gracious lord, I tender you my service, 45
Such as it is, being tender, raw, and young;
Which elder days shall ripen and confirm
To more approved service and desert.
   Boling. I thank thee, gentle Percy; and be sure
I count myself in nothing else so happy   50
As in a soul rememb'ring my good friends;
And, as my fortune ripens with thy love,
It shall be still thy true love's recompense.
My heart this covenant makes, my hand thus seals it.
   North. How far is it to Berkeley? and what stir   55
Keeps good old York there with his men of war?
   Percy. There stands the castle by yon tuft of trees,
Manned with three hundred men, as I have heard;
And in it are the Lords of York, Berkeley, and
   Seymour,   60
None else of name and noble estimate.

71. **Evermore thanks, the exchequer of the poor:** i.e., gratitude is ever the only payment the poor can make.

81. **rase:** erase.

Enter Ross and Willoughby.

North. Here come the Lords of Ross and Wil-
loughby,
Bloody with spurring, fiery red with haste.
  Boling. Welcome, my lords. I wot your love pursues 65
A banished traitor. All my treasury
Is yet but unfelt thanks, which, more enriched,
Shall be your love and labor's recompense.
  Ross. Your presence makes us rich, most noble lord.
  Wil. And far surmounts our labor to attain it. 70
  Boling. Evermore thanks, the exchequer of the poor,
Which, till my infant fortune comes to years,
Stands for my bounty. But who comes here?

Enter Berkeley.

North. It is my Lord of Berkeley, as I guess.
  Berk. My Lord of Hereford, my message is to you. 75
  Boling. My lord, my answer is—"to Lancaster";
And I am come to seek that name in England;
And I must find that title in your tongue
Before I make reply to aught you say.
  Berk. Mistake me not, my lord. 'Tis not my meaning 80
To rase one title of your honor out.
To you, my lord, I come (what lord you will)
From the most gracious Regent of this land,
The Duke of York, to know what pricks you on

90. **deceivable:** deceitful.
95. **ungracious:** graceless; wicked.
98. **more why:** another question.
101. **despised:** despicable.

To take advantage of the absent time   85
And fright our native peace with self-borne arms.

Enter York [attended].

  Boling. I shall not need transport my words by you;
Here comes His Grace in person. My noble uncle!
                                      [*Kneels.*]
  York. Show me thy humble heart, and not thy knee,
Whose duty is deceivable and false.   90
  Boling. My gracious uncle!
  York. Tut, tut!
Grace me no grace, nor uncle me no uncle.
I am no traitor's uncle, and that word "grace"
In an ungracious mouth is but profane.   95
Why have those banished and forbidden legs
Dared once to touch a dust of England's ground?
But then more why—why have they dared to march
So many miles upon her peaceful bosom,
Frighting her pale-faced villages with war   100
And ostentation of despised arms?
Comest thou because the anointed King is hence?
Why, foolish boy, the King is left behind,
And in my loyal bosom lies his power.
Were I but now the lord of such hot youth   105
As when brave Gaunt thy father and myself
Rescued the Black Prince, that young Mars of men,
From forth the ranks of many thousand French,
O, then how quickly should this arm of mine,

113. **condition:** personal characteristic.
118. **braving:** challenging; defiant.
122. **indifferent:** impartial.
134. **rouse his wrongs and chase them to the bay:** i.e., like a quarry flushed from its hiding place.
137. **distrained:** seized.

Now prisoner to the palsy, chastise thee   110
And minister correction to thy fault!
    Boling. My gracious uncle, let me know my fault;
On what condition stands it and wherein?
    York. Even in condition of the worst degree,
In gross rebellion and detested treason.   115
Thou art a banished man, and here art come,
Before the expiration of thy time,
In braving arms against thy sovereign.
    Boling. As I was banished, I was banished Hereford;
But as I come, I come for Lancaster.   120
And, noble uncle, I beseech your Grace
Look on my wrongs with an indifferent eye.
You are my father, for methinks in you
I see old Gaunt alive. O, then, my father,
Will you permit that I shall stand condemned   125
A wandering vagabond, my rights and royalties
Plucked from my arms perforce, and given away
To upstart unthrifts? Wherefore was I born?
If that my cousin king be King of England,
It must be granted I am Duke of Lancaster.   130
You have a son, Aumerle, my noble cousin.
Had you first died, and he been thus trod down,
He should have found his uncle Gaunt a father
To rouse his wrongs and chase them to the bay.
I am denied to sue my livery here,   135
And yet my letters patents give me leave.
My father's goods are all distrained and sold;
And these, and all, are all amiss employed.
What would you have me do? I am a subject,

140. **challenge law:** claim my legal rights.

144. **stands your Grace upon:** i.e., is your Grace's obligation.

149. **kind:** fashion.

150. **Be his own carver:** i.e., seize what he wants. The phrase is from the carving of meat at table.

158. **issue:** outcome.

160. **power:** army; **ill left:** poorly equipped.

162. **attach:** arrest; **stoop:** submit.

And I challenge law. Attorneys are denied me,   140
And therefore personally I lay my claim
To my inheritance of free descent.
   North. The noble Duke hath been too much abused.
   Ross. It stands your Grace upon to do him right.
   Wil. Base men by his endowments are made great.   145
   York. My lords of England, let me tell you this:
I have had feeling of my cousin's wrongs,
And labored all I could to do him right;
But in this kind to come, in braving arms,
Be his own carver and cut out his way   150
To find out right with wrong—it may not be;
And you that do abet him in this kind
Cherish rebellion and are rebels all.
   North. The noble Duke hath sworn his coming is
But for his own; and for the right of that   155
We all have strongly sworn to give him aid;
And let him never see joy that breaks that oath!
   York. Well, well, I see the issue of these arms.
I cannot mend it, I must needs confess,
Because my power is weak and all ill left;   160
But if I could, by Him that gave me life,
I would attach you all and make you stoop
Unto the sovereign mercy of the King;
But since I cannot, be it known to you
I do remain as neuter. So fare you well—   165
Unless you please to enter in the castle
And there repose you for this night.
   Boling. An offer, uncle, that we will accept;
But we must win your Grace to go with us

172. **caterpillars:** destructive parasites.

178. **things past redress are now with me past care:** proverbial: Past cure, past care.

‖‖‖‖‖‖‖‖‖‖‖‖‖‖‖‖‖‖‖‖‖‖‖‖‖‖‖‖‖‖‖‖‖‖‖‖‖‖

II. iv. The Earl of Salisbury awaits the King with a body of loyal Welsh troops. The Welsh have become disheartened by disastrous omens and fear the King is dead; Salisbury is unable to persuade them to await him longer. Salisbury himself is fearful that Richard's fortunes are declining.

‖‖‖‖‖‖‖‖‖‖‖‖‖‖‖‖‖‖‖‖‖‖‖‖‖‖‖‖‖‖

1. **stayed:** waited.

To Bristow Castle, which they say is held   170
By Bushy, Bagot, and their complices,
The caterpillars of the commonwealth,
Which I have sworn to weed and pluck away.
  York. It may be I will go with you; but yet I'll
      pause,   175
For I am loath to break our country's laws.
Nor friends nor foes, to me welcome you are.
Things past redress are now with me past care.
                                    Exeunt.

Scene IV. [A camp in Wales.]

Enter Earl of Salisbury and a Welsh Captain.

  Welsh. My Lord of Salisbury, we have stayed ten
      days
And hardly kept our countrymen together,
And yet we hear no tidings from the King.
Therefore we will disperse ourselves. Farewell.   5
  Sal. Stay yet another day, thou trusty Welshman.
The King reposeth all his confidence in thee.
  Welsh. 'Tis thought the King is dead. We will not
      stay.
The bay trees in our country are all withered,   10
And meteors fright the fixed stars of heaven;
The pale-faced moon looks bloody on the earth,
And lean-looked prophets whisper fearful change;

20. **heavy:** sorrowful.

Rich men look sad, and ruffians dance and leap—
The one in fear to lose what they enjoy,   15
The other to enjoy by rage and war.
These signs forerun the death or fall of kings.
Farewell. Our countrymen are gone and fled,
As well assured Richard their king is dead.   *Exit.*

   Sal. Ah, Richard! with the eyes of heavy mind,   20
I see thy glory, like a shooting star,
Fall to the base earth from the firmament.
Thy sun sets weeping in the lowly West,
Witnessing storms to come, woe, and unrest;
Thy friends are fled to wait upon thy foes,   25
And crossly to thy good all fortune goes.

                              Exit.

THE TRAGEDY OF
RICHARD
THE SECOND

ACT III

III. i. At Bristol, Bolingbroke takes Green and Bushy prisoner and, after charging them with misusing their influence with the King, orders their execution.

_____

3. **part:** depart.
4. **urging:** stressing.
9. **happy:** fortunate; **blood:** birth.
10. **unhappied:** made unfortunate; **disfigured:** blemished in reputation; **clean:** completely.

ACT III

‖‖

Scene I. [Bristol. Before the Castle.]

Enter Bolingbroke Duke of Hereford, York, North-
umberland, Ross, Percy, Willoughby, with Bushy and
Green prisoners.

Boling. Bring forth these men.
Bushy and Green, I will not vex your souls
(Since presently your souls must part your bodies)
With too much urging your pernicious lives,
For 'twere no charity; yet, to wash your blood   5
From off my hands, here in the view of men
I will unfold some causes of your deaths.
You have misled a prince, a royal king,
A happy gentleman in blood and lineaments,
By you unhappied and disfigured clean.   10
You have in manner with your sinful hours
Made a divorce betwixt his queen and him,
Broke the possession of a royal bed,
And stained the beauty of a fair queen's cheeks
With tears drawn from her eyes by your foul wrongs.   15
Myself—a prince by fortune of my birth,
Near to the King in blood, and near in love

20. **sighed my English breath in foreign clouds:** i.e., created vapor in foreign lands with my English breath.

22. **seigniories:** domains.

23. **Disparked:** thrown open so that they ceased to be domains reserved for private use.

24. **coat:** i.e., coat of arms.

25. **imprese:** heraldic device.

39. **entreated:** treated.

43. **at large:** in full.

Till you did make him misinterpret me—
Have stooped my neck under your injuries
And sighed my English breath in foreign clouds,   20
Eating the bitter bread of banishment,
Whilst you have fed upon my seigniories,
Disparked my parks and felled my forest woods,
From my own windows torn my household coat,
Rased out my imprese, leaving me no sign,   25
Save men's opinions and my living blood,
To show the world I am a gentleman.
This and much more, much more than twice all this,
Condemns you to the death. See them delivered over
To execution and the hand of death.   30
    Bushy. More welcome is the stroke of death to me
Than Bolingbroke to England. Lords, farewell.
    Green. My comfort is that heaven will take our
        souls
And plague injustice with the pains of hell.   35
    Boling. My Lord Northumberland, see them dis-
        patched.
        [*Exeunt Northumberland and others, with the
                                    prisoners.*]
Uncle, you say the Queen is at your house.
For God's sake, fairly let her be entreated.
Tell her I send to her my kind commends;   40
Take special care my greetings be delivered.
    York. A gentleman of mine I have dispatched
With letters of your love to her at large.
    Boling. Thanks, gentle uncle. Come, lords, away,

III. ii. The King has landed in Wales. At first confident that as God's deputy he cannot be unseated, he wavers between hope and fear as friends encourage him or report the latest bad news. When he hears that York has joined Bolingbroke, he sinks into despair and orders his forces dismissed.

||||||||||||||||||||||||||||||||

1. **Barkloughly:** an error from Holinshed for "Hertlowli" (Harlech).
2. **brooks:** endures; tolerates.
11. **do thee favors:** honor thee.
16. **annoyance:** injury.

To fight with Glendower and his complices.   45
Awhile to work, and after holiday.

Exeunt.

Scene II. [The coast of Wales. A castle in view.]

Drums. Flourish and Colors. Enter the King, Aumerle,
[the Bishop of] Carlisle, and Soldiers.

King. Barkloughly Castle call they this at hand?
Aum. Yea, my lord. How brooks your Grace the air
After your late tossing on the breaking seas?
King. Needs must I like it well. I weep for joy
To stand upon my kingdom once again.   5
Dear earth, I do salute thee with my hand,
Though rebels wound thee with their horses' hoofs.
As a long-parted mother with her child
Plays fondly with her tears and smiles in meeting,
So weeping, smiling, greet I thee, my earth,   10
And do thee favors with my royal hands.
Feed not thy sovereign's foe, my gentle earth,
Nor with thy sweets comfort his ravenous sense;
But let thy spiders that suck up thy venom,
And heavy-gaited toads, lie in their way,   15
Doing annoyance to the treacherous feet
Which with usurping steps do trample thee.
Yield stinging nettles to mine enemies;
And when they from thy bosom pluck a flower,

21. **double:** forked; **mortal:** deadly.

23. **senseless:** that is, addressed to a senseless object.

25. **native:** natural.

35. **security:** overconfidence.

37. **Discomfortable:** discouraging.

41. **boldly:** an editorial correction. The Quarto reads "bouldy," the Folio "bloody."

44. **guilty hole:** i.e., hiding place of guilt.

The hidden snake.
From Claude Paradin, *Devises heroiques* (1557).

Guard it, I pray thee, with a lurking adder　　　20
Whose double tongue may with a mortal touch
Throw death upon thy sovereign's enemies.
Mock not my senseless conjuration, lords.
This earth shall have a feeling, and these stones
Prove armed soldiers ere her native king　　　25
Shall falter under foul rebellion's arms.

　　Car. Fear not, my lord. That Power that made you
　　　　king
Hath power to keep you king in spite of all.
The means that heaven yields must be embraced,　　　30
And not neglected; else, if heaven would,
And we will not, heaven's offer we refuse,
The proffered means of succor and redress.

　　Aum. He means, my lord, that we are too remiss,
Whilst Bolingbroke, through our security,　　　35
Grows strong and great in substance and in power.

　　King. Discomfortable cousin! knowst thou not
That when the searching eye of heaven is hid
Behind the globe, that lights the lower world,
Then thieves and robbers range abroad unseen　　　40
In murders and in outrage boldly here;
But when from under this terrestrial ball
He fires the proud tops of the Eastern pines
And darts his light through every guilty hole,
Then murders, treasons, and detested sins,　　　45
The cloak of night being plucked from off their backs,
Stand bare and naked, trembling at themselves?
So when this thief, this traitor Bolingbroke,
Who all this while hath reveled in the night

50. **we:** that is, Richard himself, England's royal sun; **the Antipodes:** the inhabitants of the lower half of the earth.

57. **worldly men:** humans.

59. **pressed:** impressed; enlisted.

60. **shrewd:** hostile.

62. **angel:** with a pun on the coin of that name.

65. **Nor:** neither; **near:** the comparative of Old English *néah* (nigh). The modern "nearer" is thus a double comparative.

66. **Discomfort:** discouragement; disheartenment.

Whilst we were wand'ring with the Antipodes,   50
Shall see us rising in our throne, the East,
His treasons will sit blushing in his face,
Not able to endure the sight of day,
But self-affrighted tremble at his sin.
Not all the water in the rough rude sea   55
Can wash the balm off from an anointed king.
The breath of worldly men cannot depose
The deputy elected by the Lord.
For every man that Bolingbroke hath pressed
To lift shrewd steel against our golden crown,   60
God for his Richard hath in heavenly pay
A glorious angel. Then, if angels fight,
Weak men must fall; for heaven still guards the right.

Enter Salisbury.

Welcome, my lord. How far off lies your power?
Sal. Nor near nor farther off, my gracious lord,   65
Than this weak arm. Discomfort guides my tongue
And bids me speak of nothing but despair.
One day too late, I fear me, noble lord,
Hath clouded all thy happy days on earth.
O, call back yesterday, bid time return,   70
And thou shalt have twelve thousand fighting men!
Today, today, unhappy day too late,
O'erthrows thy joys, friends, fortune, and thy state;
For all the Welshmen, hearing thou wert dead,
Are gone to Bolingbroke, dispersed, and fled.   75

76. **Comfort:** take heart.

78–9. **the blood of twenty thousand men/Did triumph in my face:** that is, my face was flushed with triumph at the thought of the twenty thousand men at my command.

94. **betide:** befall.

95. **care-tuned:** tuned for the delivery of bad news; **deliver:** report to.

98. **care:** source of care; anxiety.

Aum. Comfort, my liege. Why looks your Grace so
    pale?

King. But now the blood of twenty thousand men
Did triumph in my face, and they are fled;
And, till so much blood thither come again,   80
Have I not reason to look pale and dead?
All souls that will be safe, fly from my side;
For time hath set a blot upon my pride.

    Aum. Comfort, my liege. Remember who you are.

    King. I had forgot myself. Am I not King?   85
Awake, thou coward majesty! thou sleepest.
Is not the King's name twenty thousand names?
Arm, arm, my name! A puny subject strikes
At thy great glory. Look not to the ground,
Ye favorites of a king. Are we not high?   90
High be our thoughts. I know my uncle York
Hath power enough to serve our turn. But who comes
    here?

Enter Scroop.

Scroop. More health and happiness betide my liege
Than can my care-tuned tongue deliver him!   95

    King. Mine ear is open and my heart prepared.
The worst is worldly loss thou canst unfold.
Say, is my kingdom lost? Why, 'twas my care;
And what loss is it to be rid of care?
Strives Bolingbroke to be as great as we?   100
Greater he shall not be; if he serve God,
We'll serve him too, and be his fellow so.

112. **limits:** boundaries.

120. **beadsmen:** aged indigents, who prayed for the souls of benefactors who maintained them.

121. **double-fatal:** fatal in being poisonous in itself and in being used for bows.

122. **distaff women:** women whose proper implement is the distaff; **bills:** long-handled weapons ending in hook-shaped blades; they were rather old-fashioned in Shakespeare's time.

129. **Measure:** travel through.

Revolt our subjects? That we cannot mend;
They break their faith to God as well as us.
Cry woe, destruction, ruin, and decay: 105
The worst is death, and Death will have his day.
   Scroop. Glad am I that your Highness is so armed
To bear the tidings of calamity.
Like an unseasonable stormy day
Which makes the silver rivers drown their shores   110
As if the world were all dissolved to tears,
So high above his limits swells the rage
Of Bolingbroke, covering your fearful land
With hard bright steel, and hearts harder than steel.
White-beards have armed their thin and hairless 115
    scalps
Against thy majesty. Boys with women's voices
Strive to speak big, and clap their female joints
In stiff unwieldy arms against thy crown.
Thy very beadsmen learn to bend their bows   120
Of double-fatal yew against thy state.
Yea, distaff women manage rusty bills
Against thy seat. Both young and old rebel,
And all goes worse than I have power to tell.
   King. Too well, too well thou tellst a tale so ill. 125
Where is the Earl of Wiltshire? Where is Bagot?
What is become of Bushy? Where is Green?
That they have let the dangerous enemy
Measure our confines with such peaceful steps?
If we prevail, their heads shall pay for it.   130
I warrant they have made peace with Bolingbroke.

141. **property:** natural characteristic.

161–62. **that small model of the barren earth/ Which serves as paste and cover to our bones:** that small portion of earth that encases our corpse.

Scroop. Peace have they made with him indeed, my
    lord.
King. O villains, vipers, damned without redemp-
    tion!   135
Dogs easily won to fawn on any man!
Snakes in my heartblood warmed that sting my heart!
Three Judases, each one thrice worse than Judas!
Would they make peace? Terrible hell make war
Upon their spotted souls for this offense!   140
Scroop. Sweet love, I see, changing his property,
Turns to the sourest and most deadly hate.
Again uncurse their souls. Their peace is made
With heads, and not with hands. Those whom you
    curse   145
Have felt the worst of death's destroying wound
And lie full low, graved in the hollow ground.
Aum. Is Bushy, Green, and the Earl of Wiltshire
    dead?
Scroop. Ay, all of them at Bristow lost their heads. 150
Aum. Where is the Duke my father with his power?
King. No matter where. Of comfort no man speak!
Let's talk of graves, of worms, and epitaphs,
Make dust our paper, and with rainy eyes
Write sorrow on the bosom of the earth.   155
Let's choose executors and talk of wills.
And yet not so—for what can we bequeath,
Save our deposed bodies to the ground?
Our lands, our lives, and all are Bolingbroke's,
And nothing can we call our own but death   160
And that small model of the barren earth

170. **antic:** jester.

171. **Scoffing:** ridiculing.

174. **self and vain conceit:** a foolish misconception of himself.

176. **humored thus:** (Death) having thus indulged his whim.

188. **prevent the ways to wail:** forestall the necessity of wailing; take action to ward off disaster.

The emperor and Death.
From Fabio Glissenti, *Discorsi morali contra il dispiacer del morir* (1600).

Which serves as paste and cover to our bones.
For God's sake let us sit upon the ground
And tell sad stories of the death of kings!
How some have been deposed, some slain in war,   165
Some haunted by the ghosts they have deposed,
Some poisoned by their wives, some sleeping killed—
All murdered; for within the hollow crown
That rounds the mortal temples of a king
Keeps Death his court; and there the antic sits,   170
Scoffing his state and grinning at his pomp;
Allowing him a breath, a little scene,
To monarchize, be feared, and kill with looks;
Infusing him with self and vain conceit,
As if this flesh which walls about our life   175
Were brass impregnable; and humored thus,
Comes at the last, and with a little pin
Bores through his castle wall, and farewell king!
Cover your heads, and mock not flesh and blood
With solemn reverence. Throw away respect,   180
Tradition, form, and ceremonious duty;
For you have but mistook me all this while.
I live with bread like you, feel want, taste grief,
Need friends. Subjected thus,
How can you say to me I am a king?   185
  Car. My lord, wise men ne'er sit and wail their
      woes,
But presently prevent the ways to wail.
To fear the foe, since fear oppresseth strength,
Gives, in your weakness, strength unto your foe,   190
And so your follies fight against yourself.

192. **to fight:** in fighting.

193. **fight and die is death destroying Death:** the mental image of Death is destroyed in the action of fighting. Cf. *Julius Cæsar*, II. ii. 334: "Cowards die many times before their deaths; The valiant never taste of death but once."

199. **change:** exchange.

207. **heavier:** more distressing.

208. **by small and small:** little by little.

213. **Upon his party:** on his side.

215. **Beshrew:** plague take.

Fear, and be slain—no worse can come to fight;
And fight and die is death destroying Death,
Where fearing dying pays Death servile breath.

 Aum. My father hath a power. Inquire of him, 195
And learn to make a body of a limb.

 King. Thou chidest me well. Proud Bolingbroke, I
  come
To change blows with thee for our day of doom.
This ague fit of fear is overblown.   200
An easy task it is to win our own.
Say, Scroop, where lies our uncle with his power?
Speak sweetly, man, although thy looks be sour.

 Scroop. Men judge by the complexion of the sky
The state and inclination of the day;   205
So may you by my dull and heavy eye:
My tongue hath but a heavier tale to say.
I play the torturer, by small and small
To lengthen out the worst that must be spoken.
Your uncle York is joined with Bolingbroke, 210
And all your Northern castles yielded up,
And all your Southern gentlemen in arms
Upon his party.

 King.   Thou hast said enough.
[*To Aumerle*] Beshrew thee, cousin, which didst lead 215
  me forth
Of that sweet way I was in to despair!
What say you now? What comfort have we now?
By heaven, I'll hate him everlastingly
That bids me be of comfort any more.   220
Go to Flint Castle; there I'll pine away;

224. **ear:** plow; cultivate.

‖‖

III. iii. Bolingbroke comes to Flint Castle to which the King has retired. He swears his loyalty and declares that he seeks only his rights in the Duchy of Lancaster; the King agrees to accompany Bolingbroke's party to London and promises to give him whatever he wishes—including his crown.

A king, woe's slave, shall kingly woe obey.
That power I have, discharge; and let them go
To ear the land that hath some hope to grow,
For I have none. Let no man speak again   225
To alter this, for counsel is but vain.
    Aum. My liege, one word.
    King.   He does me double wrong
That wounds me with the flatteries of his tongue.
Discharge my followers. Let them hence away,   230
From Richard's night to Bolingbroke's fair day.
                                        Exeunt.

Scene III. [Wales. Before Flint Castle.]

Enter, with Drum and Colors, Bolingbroke, York,
Northumberland, Attendants, [and Soldiers].

    Boling. So that by this intelligence we learn
The Welshmen are dispersed, and Salisbury
Is gone to meet the King, who lately landed
With some few private friends upon this coast.
    North. The news is very fair and good, my lord.   5
Richard not far from hence hath hid his head.
    York. It would beseem the Lord Northumberland
To say "King Richard." Alack the heavy day
When such a sacred king should hide his head!
    North. Your Grace mistakes. Only to be brief   10
Left I his title out.

15. **taking so the head:** behaving so rashly and robbing him of his title.

19. **mistake:** take wrongfully what is not yours.

36. **the breath of parley:** a distinctive trumpet call for a parley.

37. **his ruined ears:** that is, the ruined apertures of the castle.

York. The time hath been,
Would you have been so brief with him, he would
Have been so brief with you to shorten you,
For taking so the head, your whole head's length.   15
   Boling. Mistake not, uncle, further than you should.
   York. Take not, good cousin, further than you
      should,
Lest you mistake. The heavens are over our heads.
   Boling. I know it, uncle, and oppose not myself   20
Against their will. But who comes here?

Enter Percy.

Welcome, Harry. What, will not this castle yield?
   Percy. The castle royally is manned, my lord,
Against thy entrance.
   Boling. Royally?   25
Why, it contains no king?
   Percy.   Yes, my good lord,
It doth contain a king. King Richard lies
Within the limits of yon lime and stone;
And with him are the Lord Aumerle, Lord Salisbury,   30
Sir Stephen Scroop, besides a clergyman
Of holy reverence—who, I cannot learn.
   North. O, belike it is the Bishop of Carlisle.
   Boling. Noble lords,
Go to the rude ribs of that ancient castle;   35
Through brazen trumpet send the breath of parley
Into his ruined ears, and thus deliver:
Henry Bolingbroke

51. stooping duty: obeisance.

On both his knees doth kiss King Richard's hand
And sends allegiance and true faith of heart   40
To his most royal person; hither come
Even at his feet to lay my arms and power,
Provided that my banishment repealed
And lands restored again be freely granted.
If not, I'll use the advantage of my power,   45
And lay the summer's dust with show'rs of blood
Rained from the wounds of slaughtered Englishmen;
The which, how far off from the mind of Bolingbroke
It is such crimson tempest should bedrench
The fresh green lap of fair King Richard's land,   50
My stooping duty tenderly shall show.
Go signify as much, while here we march
Upon the grassy carpet of this plain.
Let's march without the noise of threat'ning drum,
That from this castle's tattered battlements   55
Our fair appointments may be well perused.
Methinks King Richard and myself should meet
With no less terror than the elements
Of fire and water when their thund'ring shock
At meeting tears the cloudy cheeks of heaven.   60
Be he the fire, I'll be the yielding water;
The rage be his, whilst on the earth I rain
My waters—on the earth, and not on him.
March on, and mark King Richard how he looks.

66. **blushing discontented sun:** i.e., the red sun that usually prophesies a stormy day.
80. **awful:** reverent.

Parle without, and answer within; then a flourish.
Enter, on the walls, [King] Richard, [the Bishop of]
Carlisle, Aumerle, Scroop, Salisbury.

See, see, King Richard doth himself appear,   65
As doth the blushing discontented sun
From out the fiery portal of the East
When he perceives the envious clouds are bent
To dim his glory and to stain the track
Of his bright passage to the Occident.   70
    York. Yet looks he like a king. Behold, his eye,
As bright as is the eagle's, lightens forth
Controlling majesty. Alack, alack, for woe,
That any harm should stain so fair a show!
    King. [To Nothumberland] We are amazed; and   75
        thus long have we stood
To watch the fearful bending of thy knee,
Because we thought ourself thy lawful king;
And if we be, how dare thy joints forget
To pay their awful duty to our presence?   80
If we be not, show us the hand of God
That hath dismissed us from our stewardship;
For well we know no hand of blood and bone
Can gripe the sacred handle of our scepter,
Unless he do profane, steal, or usurp.   85
And though you think that all, as you have done,
Have torn their souls by turning them from us
And we are barren and bereft of friends,
Yet know, my master, God omnipotent,

98. **purple:** crimson; the color of blood; **testament:** will.

117. **lineal royalties:** hereditary rights.

118. **Enfranchisement:** freedom from the sentence of banishment.

Is mustering in His clouds on our behalf   90
Armies of pestilence, and they shall strike
Your children yet unborn and unbegot
That lift your vassal hands against my head
And threat the glory of my precious crown.
Tell Bolingbroke, for yon methinks he stands,   95
That every stride he makes upon my land
Is dangerous treason. He is come to open
The purple testament of bleeding war.
But ere the crown he looks for live in peace,
Ten thousand bloody crowns of mothers' sons   100
Shall ill become the flower of England's face,
Change the complexion of her maid-pale peace
To scarlet indignation, and bedew
Her pastures' grass with faithful English blood.
   North. The King of Heaven forbid our lord the King 105
Should so with civil and uncivil arms
Be rushed upon! Thy thrice-noble cousin
Harry Bolingbroke doth humbly kiss thy hand;
And by the honorable tomb he swears
That stands upon your royal grandsire's bones,   110
And by the royalties of both your bloods
(Currents that spring from one most gracious head),
And by the buried hand of warlike Gaunt,
And by the worth and honor of himself,
Comprising all that may be sworn or said,   115
His coming hither hath no further scope
Than for his lineal royalties, and to beg
Enfranchisement immediate on his knees;
Which on thy royal party granted once,

121. **barbed:** armored.
124. **credit:** believe.
125. **returns:** replies.
127. **demands:** requests.
143. **sooth:** flattery.
144. **name:** title.

His glittering arms he will commend to rust,   120
His barbed steeds to stables, and his heart
To faithful service of your Majesty.
This swears he, as he is a prince, is just;
And as I am a gentleman, I credit him.

   King. Northumberland, say thus the King returns: 125
His noble cousin is right welcome hither;
And all the number of his fair demands
Shall be accomplished without contradiction.
With all the gracious utterance thou hast
Speak to his gentle hearing kind commends.   130
[*To Aumerle*] We do debase ourselves, cousin, do we
    not,
To look so poorly and to speak so fair?
Shall we call back Northumberland and send
Defiance to the traitor, and so die?   135

   Aum. No, good my lord. Let's fight with gentle
    words
Till time lend friends, and friends their helpful
    swords.

   King. O God, O God! that e'er this tongue of mine 140
That laid the sentence of dread banishment
On yon proud man, should take it off again
With words of sooth! O that I were as great
As is my grief, or lesser than my name!
Or that I could forget what I have been!   145
Or not remember what I must be now!
Swellst thou, proud heart? I'll give thee scope to beat,
Since foes have scope to beat both thee and me.

155. **A:** in.
160. **palmer's:** pilgrim's.
171. **lodge:** beat down; **corn:** wheat.
173–74. **play the wantons with our woes/And make some pretty match with shedding tears:** treat our sorrows sportively and make a clever jest with our tears.

Aum. Northumberland comes back from Boling-   150
  broke.
  King. What must the King do now? Must he
    submit?
The King shall do it. Must he be deposed?
The King shall be contented. Must he lose
The name of king? A God's name, let it go!   155
I'll give my jewels for a set of beads,
My gorgeous palace for a hermitage,
My gay apparel for an almsman's gown,
My figured goblets for a dish of wood,
My scepter for a palmer's walking staff,   160
My subjects for a pair of carved saints,
And my large kingdom for a little grave,
A little little grave, an obscure grave;
Or I'll be buried in the king's highway,
Some way of common trade, where subjects' feet   165
May hourly trample on their sovereign's head;
For on my heart they tread now whilst I live,
And buried once, why not upon my head?
Aumerle, thou weepst, my tenderhearted cousin!
We'll make foul weather with despised tears;   170
Our sighs and they shall lodge the summer corn
And make a dearth in this revolting land.
Or shall we play the wantons with our woes
And make some pretty match with shedding tears?
As thus—to drop them still upon one place   175
Till they have fretted us a pair of graves
Within the earth; and therein laid—there lies
Two kinsmen digged their graves with weeping eyes.

180. **idly:** foolishly.

184. **make a leg:** bend the knee; bow.

185. **base:** outer.

187. **Phaeton:** Phaeton, son of Phoebus, the sun god, insisted on driving his father's chariot across the sky and, being unable to manage the horses, was despatched by a thunderbolt from Jove when destruction of the earth was threatened by the chariot's uncontrolled course.

188. **Wanting:** lacking; **manage:** control in the technical sense of horsemanship; **jades:** nags.

190. **grace:** honor.

197. **fondly:** foolishly; **frantic:** lunatic.

200. **fair duty:** proper respect.

Phaeton.
From Geoffrey Whitney, *Choice of Emblems* (1586).

Would not this ill do well? Well, well, I see
I talk but idly, and you laugh at me.   180
Most mighty prince, my Lord Northumberland,
What says King Bolingbroke? Will His Majesty
Give Richard leave to live till Richard die?
You make a leg, and Bolingbroke says aye.
    North. My lord, in the base court he doth attend   185
To speak with you, may it please you to come down.
    King. Down, down I come, like glist'ring Phaeton,
Wanting the manage of unruly jades.
In the base court? Base court, where kings grow base,
To come at traitors' calls and do them grace!   190
In the base court? Come down? Down court! down
    king!
For night owls shriek where mounting larks should
    sing.   [*Exeunt from above.*]
    Boling. What says His Majesty?   195
    North.   Sorrow and grief of heart
Makes him speak fondly, like a frantic man.
Yet he is come.

                [*Enter King Richard attended, below.*]

    Boling. Stand all apart
And show fair duty to His Majesty. *He kneels down.*   200
My gracious lord—
    King. Fair cousin, you debase your princely knee
To make the base earth proud with kissing it.
Me rather had my heart might feel your love
Than my unpleased eye see your courtesy.   205

212. **redoubted:** formidable.

217. **Tears show their love, but want their remedies:** tears show love but cannot change the circumstances that cause them.

ııı

III. iv. The sorrowful Queen learns of the deaths of Bushy and Green and hears rumors that her husband has been deposed. She decides to go at once to London to join the King.

Up, cousin, up! Your heart is up, I know,
Thus high at least [*Touches his head*], although your
    knee be low.
  Boling. [*Rises*] My gracious lord, I come but for
    mine own.   210
  King. Your own is yours, and I am yours, and all.
  Boling. So far be mine, my most redoubted lord,
As my true service shall deserve your love.
  King. Well you deserve. They well deserve to have
That know the strong'st and surest way to get.   215
Uncle, give me your hand. Nay, dry your eyes.
Tears show their love, but want their remedies.
Cousin, I am too young to be your father,
Though you are old enough to be my heir.
What you will have, I'll give, and willing too;   220
For do we must what force will have us do.
Set on toward London. Cousin, is it so?
  Boling. Yea, my good lord.
  King.   Then I must not say no.
                         Flourish. Exeunt.

Scene IV. [Langley. The Duke of York's garden.]

Enter the Queen with two Ladies, her Attendants.

  Queen. What sport shall we devise here in this
    garden
To drive away the heavy thought of care?

6. **rubs:** obstacles; a technical term from bowling.

7. **against the bias:** another bowling term meaning "awry."

9. **measure:** rhythmical motion as of a dance.

10. **measure:** moderation.

13. **joy:** Nicholas Rowe's reading; the Quarto and Folio read "griefe."

21. **boots:** avails.

Lady. Madam, we'll play at bowls.

Queen. 'Twill make me think the world is full of   5
   rubs
And that my fortune runs against the bias.

Lady. Madam, we'll dance.

Queen. My legs can keep no measure in delight
When my poor heart no measure keeps in grief.   10
Therefore no dancing, girl; some other sport.

Lady. Madam, we'll tell tales.

Queen. Of sorrow or of joy?

Lady.   Of either, madam.

Queen. Of neither, girl;   15
For if of joy, being altogether wanting,
It doth remember me the more of sorrow;
Or if of grief, being altogether had,
It adds more sorrow to my want of joy;
For what I have I need not to repeat,   20
And what I want it boots not to complain.

Lady. Madam, I'll sing.

Queen.   'Tis well that thou hast cause;
But thou shouldst please me better wouldst thou
   weep.   25

Lady. I could weep, madam, would it do you good.

Queen. And I could sing, would weeping do me
   good,
And never borrow any tear of thee.

32. My wretchedness unto a row of pins: i.e., I'll wager my great misery against a mere row of pins.

34. Against a change: when a change is imminent.

44. noisome: poisonous.

46. in the compass of a pale: within an enclosure, referring to the walled-in garden.

52. knots: flowerbeds planted in intricate patterns; knot gardens.

55. suffered: permitted.

Enter a Gardener and two Servants.

But stay, here come the gardeners.   30
Let's step into the shadow of these trees.
My wretchedness unto a row of pins,
They will talk of state, for everyone doth so
Against a change: woe is forerun with woe.
                    [*Queen and Ladies step aside.*]
  Gard. Go bind thou up yon dangling apricocks,   35
Which, like unruly children, make their sire
Stoop with oppression of their prodigal weight.
Give some supportance to the bending twigs.
Go thou and, like an executioner,
Cut off the heads of too fast growing sprays   40
That look too lofty in our commonwealth.
All must be even in our government.
You thus employed, I will go root away
The noisome weeds which without profit suck
The soil's fertility from wholesome flowers.   45
  Man. Why should we, in the compass of a pale,
Keep law and form and due proportion,
Showing, as in a model, our firm estate,
When our sea-walled garden, the whole land,
Is full of weeds, her fairest flowers choked up,   50
Her fruit trees all unpruned, her hedges ruined,
Her knots disordered, and her wholesome herbs
Swarming with caterpillars?
  Gard.   Hold thy peace.
He that hath suffered this disordered spring   55

68. **overproud:** too luxuriant.

69. **confound:** destroy.

78. **doubt:** fear.

81–2. **pressed to death through want of speaking:** a reference to the penalty of *peine forte et dure*, crushing under weights applied to an accused person who refused to plead.

83. **dress:** cultivate.

From Thomas Hill, *The Gardener's Labyrinth* (1577).

Hath now himself met with the fall of leaf.
The weeds which his broad-spreading leaves did
    shelter,
That seemed in eating him to hold him up,
Are plucked up root and all by Bolingbroke: 60
I mean the Earl of Wiltshire, Bushy, Green.
   Man. What, are they dead?
   Gard.   They are; and Bolingbroke
Hath seized the wasteful King. O, what pity is it
That he had not so trimmed and dressed his land   65
As we this garden! We at time of year
Do wound the bark, the skin of our fruit trees,
Lest, being overproud in sap and blood,
With too much riches it confound itself.
Had he done so to great and growing men,   70
They might have lived to bear, and he to taste
Their fruits of duty. Superfluous branches
We lop away, that bearing boughs may live.
Had he done so, himself had borne the crown,
Which waste of idle hours hath quite thrown down.   75
   Man. What, think you the King shall be deposed?
   Gard. Depressed he is already, and deposed
'Tis doubt he will be. Letters came last night
To a dear friend of the good Duke of York's
That tell black tidings.   80
   Queen. O, I am pressed to death through want of
    speaking!   [*Coming forward.*]
Thou old Adam's likeness, set to dress this garden,
How dares thy harsh rude tongue sound this un-
    pleasing news?   85

86. **suggested:** tempted.

95. **weighed:** balanced against each other.

97. **vanities that make him light:** follies that lessen his reputation.

104. **Doth not thy embassage belong to me:** does not your message concern me particularly.

110. **triumph:** triumphal procession.

111. **these news:** news was quite commonly a plural, since like the Latin *res novae* it meant "new things."

What Eve, what serpent, hath suggested thee
To make a second fall of cursed man?
Why dost thou say King Richard is deposed?
Darest thou, thou little better thing than earth,
Divine his downfall? Say, where, when, and how   90
Camest thou by this ill tidings? Speak, thou wretch!
   Gard. Pardon me, madam. Little joy have I
To breathe this news; yet what I say is true.
King Richard, he is in the mighty hold
Of Bolingbroke. Their fortunes both are weighed.   95
In your lord's scale is nothing but himself,
And some few vanities that make him light;
But in the balance of great Bolingbroke,
Besides himself, are all the English peers,
And with that odds he weighs King Richard down.   100
Post you to London, and you will find it so.
I speak no more than everyone doth know.
   Queen. Nimble mischance, that art so light of foot,
Doth not thy embassage belong to me,
And am I last that knows it? O thou thinkest   105
To serve me last, that I may longest keep
Thy sorrow in my breast. Come, ladies, go
To meet at London London's king in woe.
What, was I born to this, that my sad look
Should grace the triumph of great Bolingbroke?   110
Gard'ner, for telling me these news of woe,
Pray God the plants thou graftst may never grow.
                       Exit [with Ladies].
   Gard. Poor Queen, so that thy state might be no
    worse,

117. **sour:** bitter; **herb of grace:** so called because rue (repentance) was attributed to God's grace.

118. **ruth:** compassion.

A knot garden.
From Thomas Hill, *The Gardener's Labyrinth* (1577).

I would my skill were subject to thy curse! 115
Here did she fall a tear; here in this place
I'll set a bank of rue, sour herb of grace.
Rue, even for ruth, here shortly shall be seen,
In the remembrance of a weeping queen.

                                        Exeunt.

THE TRAGEDY OF
RICHARD
THE SECOND

ACT IV

IV. i. In London, Bolingbroke questions Bagot about the death of Gloucester. Bagot accuses Aumerle and is seconded by several others. One, Fitzwater, quotes Norfolk as accusing Aumerle. Bolingbroke declares that Norfolk will be recalled from banishment but is told that he is dead. Having ordered a day of trial to be set for the lords to settle the dispute by combat, Bolingbroke is joined by York, who reports that Richard is willing to name him his heir and yield his scepter to him. The Bishop of Carlisle objects when Bolingbroke ascends the throne and Northumberland arrests the Bishop as a traitor.

The submissive but self-pitying King is summoned and states his willingness to abdicate in favor of Bolingbroke. A day for the coronation is set and the King is ordered to be conveyed to the Tower. The Abbot of Westminster, the Bishop of Carlisle, and Aumerle, however, are not content and plot to prevent the change of monarchs.

⁞⁞⁞⁞⁞⁞⁞⁞⁞⁞⁞⁞⁞⁞⁞⁞⁞⁞⁞⁞⁞⁞⁞⁞⁞⁞⁞⁞

4. **wrought:** worked, in the sense either of influencing the King to order the murder or actually participating in the deed.

5. **timeless:** untimely.

12. **dead:** fatal.

ACT IV

⸻

Scene I. [Westminster Hall.]

*Enter, as to the Parliament, Bolingbroke, Aumerle,
Northumberland, Percy, Fitzwater, Surrey, [and
another Lord, the Bishop of] Carlisle, Abbot of Westminster, Herald; Officers and Bagot.*

Boling. Call forth Bagot.
　　　　　　　　　　[Bagot is brought forward.]
Now, Bagot, freely speak thy mind
What thou dost know of noble Gloucester's death;
Who wrought it with the King, and who performed
The bloody office of his timeless end.　　　　　　5
　Bagot. Then set before my face the Lord Aumerle.
　Boling. Cousin, stand forth, and look upon that
　　man.
　Bagot. My Lord Aumerle, I know your daring
　　tongue　　　　　　　　　　　　　　　　　　10
Scorns to unsay what once it hath delivered.
In that dead time when Gloucester's death was
　　plotted,
I heard you say, "Is not my arm of length,
That reacheth from the restful English court　　15
As far as Calais to mine uncle's head?"

76

20. **Bolingbroke's return:** i.e., than see Bolingbroke return.

25. **fair stars:** good fortune, with particular reference to his noble birth.

28. **attainder:** dishonoring allegation; shameful accusation.

29. **manual seal of death:** death warrant.

35. **one:** that is, Bolingbroke; **best:** most noble.

37. **stand on sympathy:** insist on correspondence in rank.

40. **vauntingly:** boastfully.

Amongst much other talk that very time
I heard you say that you had rather refuse
The offer of an hundred thousand crowns
Than Bolingbroke's return to England;   20
Adding withal, how blest this land would be
In this your cousin's death.

   Aum.   Princes and noble lords,
What answer shall I make to this base man?
Shall I so much dishonor my fair stars   25
On equal terms to give him chastisement?
Either I must, or have mine honor soiled
With the attainder of his slanderous lips.
There is my gage, the manual seal of death
That marks thee out for hell. I say thou liest,   30
And will maintain what thou hast said is false
In thy heartblood, though being all too base
To stain the temper of my knightly sword.

   Boling. Bagot, forbear; thou shalt not take it up.

   Aum. Excepting one, I would he were the best   35
In all this presence that hath moved me so.

   Fitz. If that thy valor stand on sympathy,
There is my gage, Aumerle, in gage to thine.
By that fair sun which shows me where thou standst,
I heard thee say, and vauntingly thou spakest it,   40
That thou wert cause of noble Gloucester's death.
If thou deniest it twenty times, thou liest,
And I will turn thy falsehood to thy heart,
Where it was forged, with my rapier's point.

   Aum. Thou darest not, coward, live to see that day.   45

49. **all unjust:** completely dishonest.

56. **task thee:** Capell's emendation. The Quarto reads "task the earth." **Task** means challenge.

60. **pawn:** pledge.

61. **Engage it to the trial:** i.e., regard it as my gage that I challenge you to answer in combat.

62. **Who sets me else:** who else challenges me. To **set** is literally to put up a stake in a dice game; **throw at all:** take on all comers; another term from dicing.

Fitz. Now, by my soul, I would it were this hour.

Aum. Fitzwater, thou art damned to hell for this.

Percy. Aumerle, thou liest. His honor is as true
In this appeal as thou art all unjust;
And that thou art so, there I throw my gage　　50
To prove it on thee to the extremest point
Of mortal breathing. Seize it if thou darest.

Aum. And if I do not, may my hands rot off
And never brandish more revengeful steel
Over the glittering helmet of my foe!　　55

Another Lord. I task thee to the like, forsworn
　　Aumerle;
And spur thee on with full as many lies
As may be holloaed in thy treacherous ear
From sun to sun. There is my honor's pawn.　　60
Engage it to the trial, if thou darest.

Aum. Who sets me else? By heaven, I'll throw at all!
I have a thousand spirits in one breast
To answer twenty thousand such as you.

Surrey. My Lord Fitzwater, I do remember well　　65
The very time Aumerle and you did talk.

Fitz. 'Tis very true. You were in presence then,
And you can witness with me this is true.

Surrey. As false, by heaven, as heaven itself is true!

Fitz. Surrey, thou liest.　　70

Surrey. 　　　　　　　Dishonorable boy!
That lie shall lie so heavy on my sword
That it shall render vengeance and revenge
Till thou the lie-giver and that lie do lie
In earth as quiet as thy father's skull.　　75

78. **fondly:** foolishly; **forward:** eager.

80. **in a wilderness:** i.e., where we will be at each other's mercy.

84. **this new world:** the new order to be instituted by Bolingbroke.

102. **toiled:** wearied.

In proof whereof there is my honor's pawn.
Engage it to the trial if thou darest.
  Fitz. How fondly dost thou spur a forward horse!
If I dare eat, or drink, or breathe, or live,
I dare meet Surrey in a wilderness,   80
And spit upon him whilst I say he lies,
And lies, and lies. There is my bond of faith
To tie thee to my strong correction.
As I intend to thrive in this new world,
Aumerle is guilty of my true appeal.   85
Besides, I heard the banished Norfolk say
That thou, Aumerle, didst send two of thy men
To execute the noble Duke at Calais.
  Aum. Some honest Christian trust me with a gage
That Norfolk lies. Here do I throw down this,   90
If he may be repealed to try his honor.
  Boling. These differences shall all rest under gage
Till Norfolk be repealed. Repealed he shall be
And, though mine enemy, restored again
To all his lands and seigniories. When he's returned,   95
Against Aumerle we will enforce his trial.
  Car. That honorable day shall ne'er be seen.
Many a time hath banished Norfolk fought
For Jesu Christ in glorious Christian field,
Streaming the ensign of the Christian cross   100
Against black pagans, Turks, and Saracens;
And, toiled with works of war, retired himself
To Italy; and there at Venice gave
His body to that pleasant country's earth

115. **plume-plucked:** humbled.

121. **Marry:** by the Virgin Mary.

122. **Worst:** lowest in rank.

123. **best beseeming me to speak the truth:** that is, as a churchman it best becomes me to speak the truth.

126. **noblesse:** nobility.

127. **Learn:** teach; **forbearance:** abstention.

130. **but they are by:** i.e., except in their presence.

131. **apparent:** obvious; undoubted.

And his pure soul unto his captain, Christ,   105
Under whose colors he had fought so long.
     Boling. Why, Bishop, is Norfolk dead?
     Car. As surely as I live, my lord.
     Boling. Sweet peace conduct his sweet soul to the
          bosom   110
Of good old Abraham! Lords appellants,
Your differences shall all rest under gage
Till we assign you to your days of trial.

Enter York [attended].

     York. Great Duke of Lancaster, I come to thee
From plume-plucked Richard, who with willing soul 115
Adopts thee heir and his high scepter yields
To the possession of thy royal hand.
Ascend his throne, descending now from him,
And long live Henry, fourth of that name!
     Boling. In God's name I'll ascend the regal throne. 120
     Car. Marry, God forbid!
Worst in this royal presence may I speak,
Yet best beseeming me to speak the truth.
Would God that any in this noble presence
Were enough noble to be upright judge   125
Of noble Richard! then true noblesse would
Learn him forbearance from so foul a wrong.
What subject can give sentence on his king?
And who sits here that is not Richard's subject?
Thieves are not judged but they are by to hear,   130
Although apparent guilt be seen in them;

136. **forfend:** forbid.

148. **kind with kind confound:** i.e., men of the same race destroy each other.

151. **Golgotha:** Calvary, the site of the Crucifixion.

And shall the figure of God's majesty,
His captain, steward, deputy elect,
Anointed, crowned, planted many years,
Be judged by subject and inferior breath,   135
And he himself not present? O, forfend it, God
That, in a Christian climate, souls refined
Should show so heinous, black, obscene a deed!
I speak to subjects, and a subject speaks,
Stirred up by God, thus boldly for his king.   140
My Lord of Hereford here, whom you call king,
Is a foul traitor to proud Hereford's king;
And if you crown him, let me prophesy,
The blood of English shall manure the ground
And future ages groan for this foul act;   145
Peace shall go sleep with Turks and infidels,
And in this seat of peace tumultuous wars
Shall kin with kin and kind with kind confound;
Disorder, horror, fear, and mutiny
Shall here inhabit, and this land be called   150
The field of Golgotha and dead men's skulls.
O, if you raise this house against this house,
It will the woefullest division prove
That ever fell upon this cursed earth.
Prevent it, resist it, let it not be so,   155
Lest child, child's children cry against you woe.
    North. Well have you argued, sir; and for your
        pains
Of capital treason we arrest you here.
My Lord of Westminster, be it your charge   160

162–335. **May . . . fall:** this passage was omitted from the first three Quartos, presumably because of government censorship. Our text is taken from the Fourth Quarto and the First Folio.

166. **conduct:** escort.

177. **favors:** features.

178. **sometime:** at one time; formerly.

To keep him safely till his day of trial.
May it please you, lords, to grant the commons' suit.
    Boling. Fetch hither Richard, that in common view
He may surrender. So we shall proceed
Without suspicion.   165
    York.   I will be his conduct.   *Exit.*
    Boling. Lords, you that here are under our arrest,
Procure your sureties for your days of answer.
Little are we beholding to your love,
And little looked for at your helping hands.   170

*Enter Richard and York, [with Officers bearing the
                    regalia].*

    Rich. Alack, why am I sent for to a king
Before I have shook off the regal thoughts
Wherewith I reigned? I hardly yet have learned
To insinuate, flatter, bow, and bend my knee.
Give sorrow leave awhile to tutor me   175
To this submission. Yet I well remember
The favors of these men. Were they not mine?
Did they not sometime cry "All hail!" to me?
So Judas did to Christ; but he, in twelve,
Found truth in all but one; I, in twelve thousand, 180
    none.
God save the King! Will no man say amen?
Am I both priest and clerk? Well then, amen!
God save the King! although I be not he;
And yet amen, if heaven do think him me.   185
To do what service am I sent for hither?

196. **owes:** possesses.

212. **tend:** attend.

214. **Aye:** pronounced like the pronoun "I" and used here as a pun on the pronoun.

216. **undo:** unmake.

York. To do that office of thine own good will
Which tired majesty did make thee offer:
The resignation of thy state and crown
To Henry Bolingbroke.   190
   Rich. Give me the crown. Here, cousin, seize the
    crown.
Here, cousin,
On this side my hand, and on that side thine.
Now is this golden crown like a deep well   195
That owes two buckets, filling one another,
The emptier ever dancing in the air,
The other down, unseen, and full of water.
That bucket down and full of tears am I,
Drinking my griefs whilst you mount up on high.   200
   Boling. I thought you had been willing to resign.
   Rich. My crown I am, but still my griefs are mine.
You may my glories and my state depose,
But not my griefs; still am I king of those.
   Boling. Part of your cares you give me with your   205
    crown.
   Rich. Your cares set up do not pluck my cares
    down.
My care is loss of care, by old care done;
Your care is gain of care, by new care won.   210
The cares I give I have, though given away;
They tend the crown, yet still with me they stay.
   Boling. Are you contented to resign the crown?
   Rich. Aye, no; no, aye; for I must nothing be;
Therefore no no, for I resign to thee.   215
Now mark me how I will undo myself.

219. **sway:** rule.

220. **balm:** i.e., the oil with which he was anointed at his coronation.

239. **state and profit:** profitable state.

I give this heavy weight from off my head
And this unwieldy scepter from my hand,
The pride of kingly sway from out my heart.
With mine own tears I wash away my balm,   220
With mine own hands I give away my crown,
With mine own tongue deny my sacred state,
With mine own breath release all duteous oaths.
All pomp and majesty I do forswear:
My manors, rents, revenues I forgo;   225
My acts, decrees, and statutes I deny.
God pardon all oaths that are broke to me!
God keep all vows unbroke that swear to thee!
Make me, that nothing have, with nothing grieved,
And thou with all pleased, that hast all achieved!   230
Long mayst thou live in Richard's seat to sit,
And soon lie Richard in an earthy pit!
God save King Harry, unkinged Richard says,
And send him many years of sunshine days!
What more remains?   235
   North.   No more, but that you read
These accusations and these grievous crimes
Committed by your person and your followers
Against the state and profit of this land,
That, by confessing them, the souls of men   240
May deem that you are worthily deposed.
   Rich. Must I do so? and must I ravel out
My weaved-up folly? Gentle Northumberland,
If thy offenses were upon record,
Would it not shame thee in so fair a troop   245
To read a lecture of them? If thou wouldst,

260. **sort:** company.

268. **haught:** haughty.

270. **not that name was given me at the font:** i.e., not even my christened name. Arguing from his belief in the sanctity of sovereignty, Richard feels that if he is not King he is nothing.

There shouldst thou find one heinous article,
Containing the deposing of a king
And cracking the strong warrant of an oath,
Marked with a blot, damned in the book of heaven.   250
Nay, all of you that stand and look upon
Whilst that my wretchedness doth bait myself,
Though some of you, with Pilate, wash your hands,
Showing an outward pity, yet you Pilates
Have here delivered me to my sour cross,   255
And water cannot wash away your sin.
   North. My lord, dispatch. Read o'er these articles.
   Rich. Mine eyes are full of tears; I cannot see.
And yet salt water blinds them not so much
But they can see a sort of traitors here.   260
Nay, if I turn mine eyes upon myself,
I find myself a traitor with the rest;
For I have given here my soul's consent
To undeck the pompous body of a king;
Made glory base, and sovereignty a slave,   265
Proud majesty a subject, state a peasant.
   North. My lord—
   Rich. No lord of thine, thou haught insulting man,
Nor no man's lord. I have no name, no title—
No, not that name was given me at the font—   270
But 'tis usurped. Alack the heavy day,
That I have worn so many winters out
And know not now what name to call myself!
O that I were a mockery king of snow,
Standing before the sun of Bolingbroke,   275
To melt myself away in water drops!

278. **be sterling:** have currency.
279. **straight:** immediately.
281. **his:** its.
299. **wink:** blink.

Good king, great king, and yet not greatly good,
An if my word be sterling yet in England,
Let it command a mirror hither straight,
That it may show me what a face I have   280
Since it is bankrout of his majesty.

   Boling. Go some of you and fetch a looking glass.
                               [Exit an Attendant.]
   North. Read o'er this paper while the glass doth
     come.
   Rich. Fiend, thou torments me ere I come to hell! 285
   Boling. Urge it no more, my Lord Northumberland.
   North. The commons will not then be satisfied.
   Rich. They shall be satisfied. I'll read enough
When I do see the very book indeed
Where all my sins are writ, and that's myself.   290

Enter one with a glass.

Give me the glass, and therein will I read.
No deeper wrinkles yet? Hath sorrow struck
So many blows upon this face of mine
And made no deeper wounds? O flattering glass,
Like to my followers in prosperity,   295
Thou dost beguile me! Was this face the face
That every day under his household roof
Did keep ten thousand men? Was this the face
That like the sun did make beholders wink?
Was this the face that faced so many follies   300
And was at last outfaced by Bolingbroke?

302. **brittle:** fragile.
308. **shadow:** image.

A brittle glory shineth in this face.
As brittle as the glory is the face,

        [Dashes the glass against the ground.]

For there it is, cracked in a hundred shivers.
Mark, silent king, the moral of this sport—   305
How soon my sorrow hath destroyed my face.

  Boling. The shadow of your sorrow hath destroyed
The shadow of your face.

  Rich.   Say that again.
The shadow of my sorrow? Ha! let's see!   310
'Tis very true: my grief lies all within;
And these external manners of laments
Are merely shadows to the unseen grief
That swells with silence in the tortured soul.
There lies the substance; and I thank thee, king,   315
For thy great bounty that not only givest
Me cause to wail, but teachest me the way
How to lament the cause. I'll beg one boon,
And then be gone and trouble you no more.
Shall I obtain it?   320

  Boling.   Name it, fair cousin.

  Rich. Fair cousin? I am greater than a king;
For when I was a king, my flatterers
Were then but subjects; being now a subject,
I have a king here to my flatterer.   325
Being so great, I have no need to beg.

  Boling. Yet ask.

  Rich. And shall I have?

  Boling. You shall.

  Rich. Then give me leave to go.   330

334. **Conveyers:** thieves.

345. **take the sacrament:** swear on the sacrament.

351. **merry:** cheerful.

Boling. Whither?

Rich. Whither you will, so I were from your sights.

Boling. Go some of you, convey him to the Tower.

Rich. O, good! Convey? Conveyers are you all,

That rise thus nimbly by a true king's fall.   335

       [*Exit Richard, with some Lords and a Guard.*]

Boling. On Wednesday next we solemnly set down

Our coronation. Lords, prepare yourselves.

       Exeunt. Manent [*the Abbot of*] *Westminster,*

          [*the Bishop of*] *Carlisle, Aumerle.*

Abbot. A woeful pageant have we here beheld.

Car. The woe's to come. The children yet unborn

Shall feel this day as sharp to them as thorn.   340

Aum. You holy clergymen, is there no plot

To rid the realm of this pernicious blot?

Abbot. My lord,

Before I freely speak my mind herein,

You shall not only take the sacrament   345

To bury mine intents, but also to effect

Whatever I shall happen to devise.

I see your brows are full of discontent,

Your hearts of sorrow, and your eyes of te**ars.**

Come home with me to supper. I will lay   350

A plot shall show us all a merry day.

                    Exeunt.

THE TRAGEDY OF

RICHARD
THE SECOND

ACT V

V. i. The Queen has a farewell meeting with the King outside the Tower. Her pleas to be allowed to accompany her husband are in vain. Arrangements have been made to return her to her native France; the King is to be imprisoned in Pomfret Castle.

◄▮▮▮▮▮▮▮▮▮▮▮▮▮▮▮▮▮▮▮▮▮▮▮▮▮▮▮

3. **Julius Cæsar's ill-erected tower:** early historians mistakenly attributed the building of the Tower to Julius Cæsar. The Queen calls it **ill-erected** because it had been the scene of many imprisonments and executions.

12. **thou the model where old Troy did stand:** likening Richard in his humbled state to the ruins of the once mighty Troy.

13. **map:** mere picture (of what you were formerly).

15. **hard-favored:** hard-featured; ugly.

ACT V

Scene I. [London. A street leading to the Tower.]

Enter the Queen with Ladies, her Attendants.

Queen. This way the King will come. This is the
    way
To Julius Cæsar's ill-erected tower,
To whose flint bosom my condemned lord
Is doomed a prisoner by proud Bolingbroke.   5
Here let us rest, if this rebellious earth
Have any resting for her true king's queen.

Enter Richard and Guard.

But soft, but see, or rather do not see,
My fair rose wither. Yet look up, behold,
That you in pity may dissolve to dew   10
And wash him fresh again with truelove tears.
Ah, thou the model where old Troy did stand,
Thou map of honor, thou King Richard's tomb,
And not King Richard! Thou most beauteous inn,
Why should hard-favored grief be lodged in thee   15
When triumph is become an alehouse guest?

17. **Join not with grief:** i.e., do not add more distress to what I already feel.

24. **religious house:** convent.

40. **sometime:** former.

45. **betid:** happened; past.

46. **quite:** requite; pay in kind; **griefs:** sorrowful stories.

The ruins of Troy.
From Pierre Belon, *Observations de plusieurs singularitez* (1558).

Rich. Join not with grief, fair woman, do not so,
To make my end too sudden. Learn, good soul,
To think our former state a happy dream;
From which awaked, the truth of what we are   20
Shows us but this. I am sworn brother, sweet,
To grim Necessity, and he and I
Will keep a league till death. Hie thee to France
And cloister thee in some religious house.
Our holy lives must win a new world's crown,   25
Which our profane hours here have stricken down.
    Queen. What, is my Richard both in shape and
      mind
Transformed and weak'ned? Hath Bolingbroke
    deposed   30
Thine intellect? Hath he been in thy heart?
The lion dying thrusteth forth his paw
And wounds the earth, if nothing else, with rage
To be o'erpowered; and wilt thou, pupil-like,
Take thy correction, mildly kiss the rod,   35
And fawn on rage with base humility,
Which art a lion and the king of beasts?
    Rich. A king of beasts indeed! If aught but beasts,
I had been still a happy king of men.
Good sometime queen, prepare thee hence for France. 40
Think I am dead, and that even here thou takest,
As from my deathbed, thy last living leave.
In winter's tedious nights sit by the fire
With good old folks, and let them tell thee tales
Of woeful ages long ago betid;   45
And ere thou bid good night, to quite their griefs

49. **For why:** because.

56. **Pomfret:** Pontefract Castle in Yorkshire.

57. **there is order ta'en:** arrangements have been made.

65. **helping him:** having helped him.

66. **And:** added by Nicholas Rowe; not in Quarto or Folio.

70. **converts:** changes.

72. **worthy:** deserved.

Tell thou the lamentable tale of me,
And send the hearers weeping to their beds.
For why, the senseless brands will sympathize
The heavy accent of thy moving tongue   50
And in compassion weep the fire out;
And some will mourn in ashes, some coal-black,
For the deposing of a rightful king.

Enter Northumberland [attended].

North. My lord, the mind of Bolingbroke is
    changed.   55
You must to Pomfret, not unto the Tower.
And, madam, there is order ta'en for you:
With all swift speed you must away to France.
    Rich. Northumberland, thou ladder wherewithal
The mounting Bolingbroke ascends my throne,   60
The time shall not be many hours of age
More than it is ere foul sin gathering head
Shall break into corruption. Thou shalt think,
Though he divide the realm and give thee half,
It is too little, helping him to all.   65
And he shall think that thou, which knowst the way
To plant unrightful kings, wilt know again,
Being ne'er so little urged, another way
To pluck him headlong from the usurped throne.
The love of wicked men converts to fear;   70
That fear to hate, and hate turns one or both
To worthy danger and deserved death.

74. **Take leave:** say your good-bys; **must part:** must depart.

81. **pines the clime:** wastes away the land.

84. **Hallowmas:** November 1; the feast of All Hallows.

93. **ne'er the near:** i.e., no nearer. Probably Richard means that they would be kept apart even if she stayed in England.

99. **piece:** lengthen.

North. My guilt be on my head, and there an end!
Take leave and part, for you must part forthwith.

   Rich. Doubly divorced! Bad men, you violate   75
A twofold marriage: 'twixt my crown and me,
And then betwixt me and my married wife.
Let me unkiss the oath 'twixt thee and me;
And yet not so, for with a kiss 'twas made.
Part us, Northumberland—I toward the North,   80
Where shivering cold and sickness pines the clime;
My wife to France, from whence, set forth in pomp,
She came adorned hither like sweet May,
Sent back like Hallowmas or short'st of day.

   Queen. And must we be divided? Must we part?   85

   Rich. Aye, hand from hand, my love, and heart from
     heart.

   Queen. Banish us both, and send the King with me.

   North. That were some love, but little policy.

   Queen. Then whither he goes, thither let me go.   90

   Rich. So two, together weeping, make one woe.
Weep thou for me in France, I for thee here.
Better far off than, near, be ne'er the near.
Go, count thy way with sighs; I mine with groans.

   Queen. So longest way shall have the longest   95
     moans.

   Rich. Twice for one step I'll groan, the way being
     short,
And piece the way out with a heavy heart.
Come, come, in wooing sorrow let's be brief,   100
Since, wedding it, there is such length in grief.

109. **We make woe wanton:** i.e., we will spoil woe as though it were a petted child; **fond:** doting.

━━━━━━━━━━━━━━━━━━━

V. ii. Old York learns of his son Aumerle's involvement in a plot against the new King and sets off to denounce him. The Duchess of York urges her son to follow and beg the King's forgiveness.

━━━━━━━━━━━━━━━━━━━

6. **misgoverned:** unruly.
10. **Which his aspiring rider seemed to know:** that is, the steed's spirit was in keeping with his rider's ambition.

One kiss shall stop our mouths, and dumbly part.
Thus give I mine, and thus take I thy heart.
   Queen. Give me mine own again. 'Twere no good
    part   105
To take on me to keep and kill thy heart.
So, now I have mine own again, be gone,
That I may strive to kill it with a groan.
   Rich. We make woe wanton with this fond delay.
Once more adieu! The rest let sorrow say.   110
                           Exeunt.

Scene II. [London. The Duke of York's Palace.]

Enter Duke of York and the Duchess.

   Duch. My lord, you told me you would tell the rest,
When weeping made you break the story off,
Of our two cousins' coming into London.
   York. Where did I leave?
   Duch.   At that sad stop, my lord,   5
Where rude misgoverned hands from windows' tops
Threw dust and rubbish on King Richard's head.
   York. Then, as I said, the Duke, great Bolingbroke,
Mounted upon a hot and fiery steed
Which his aspiring rider seemed to know,   10
With slow but stately pace kept on his course,
Whilst all tongues cried "God save thee, Boling-
    broke!"

18. **painted imagery:** a reference to the painted hangings that were hung out along the routes of triumphal processions.

21. **lower:** that is, inclining his head humbly.

36. **badges:** symbols.

41. **bound:** limit.

You would have thought the very windows spake,
So many greedy looks of young and old   15
Through casements darted their desiring eyes
Upon his visage; and that all the walls
With painted imagery had said at once
"Jesu preserve thee! Welcome, Bolingbroke!"
Whilst he, from the one side to the other turning,   20
Bareheaded, lower than his proud steed's neck,
Bespake them thus, "I thank you, countrymen."
And thus still doing, thus he passed along.

   Duch. Alack, poor Richard! Where rode he the
     whilst?   25

   York. As in a theatre the eyes of men,
After a well-graced actor leaves the stage,
Are idly bent on him that enters next,
Thinking his prattle to be tedious,
Even so, or with much more contempt, men's eyes   30
Did scowl on Richard. No man cried "God save him!"
No joyful tongue gave him his welcome home,
But dust was thrown upon his sacred head;
Which with such gentle sorrow he shook off,
His face still combating with tears and smiles   35
(The badges of his grief and patience),
That, had not God for some strong purpose steeled
The hearts of men, they must perforce have melted
And barbarism itself have pitied him.
But heaven hath a hand in these events,   40
To whose high will we bound our calm contents.
To Bolingbroke are we sworn subjects now,
Whose state and honor I for aye allow.

45. **Aumerle that was:** he had been made Duke of Albemarle (Shakespeare's "Aumerle") by King Richard, but was stripped of his dukedom by Bolingbroke and reassumed the title of Earl of Rutland.

50. **violets:** i.e., royal favorites.

54. **bear you:** conduct yourself.

57–8. **Do these justs and triumphs hold:** are the tournaments and spectacles going forward as planned.

62. **seal:** the seal of the document was placed on a separate strip attached to the bottom of the paper.

Enter Aumerle.

Duch. Here comes my son Aumerle.

York.   Aumerle that was;   45
But that is lost for being Richard's friend,
And, madam, you must call him Rutland now.
I am in parliament pledge for his truth
And lasting fealty to the new-made king.

Duch. Welcome, my son. Who are the violets now   50
That strew the green lap of the new-come spring?

Aum. Madam, I know not, nor I greatly care not.
God knows I had as lief be none as one.

York. Well, bear you well in this new spring of
    time,   55
Lest you be cropped before you come to prime.
What news from Oxford? Do these justs and triumphs
    hold?

Aum. For aught I know, my lord, they do.

York. You will be there, I know.   60

Aum. If God prevent not, I purpose so.

York. What seal is that that hangs without thy
    bosom?
Yea, lookst thou pale? Let me see the writing.

Aum. My lord, 'tis nothing.   65

York.   No matter then who see it.
I will be satisfied; let me see the writing.

Aum. I do beseech your Grace to pardon me.
It is a matter of small consequence
Which for some reasons I would not have seen.   70

81. **be satisfied:** ascertain the truth.
90. **appeach:** inform against.

York. Which for some reasons, sir, I mean to see.
I fear, I fear—
    Duch.   What should you fear?
'Tis nothing but some bond that he is ent'red into
For gay apparel 'gainst the triumph day.   75
    York. Bound to himself? What doth he with a bond
That he is bound to? Wife, thou art a fool.
Boy, let me see the writing.
    Aum. I do beseech you pardon me. I may not show
      it.   80
    York. I will be satisfied. Let me see it, I say.
            He plucks it out of his bosom and reads it.
Treason, foul treason! Villain! traitor! slave!
    Duch. What is the matter, my lord?
    York. Ho! who is within there?

            [*Enter a Servant.*]

                        Saddle my horse.   85
God for his mercy, what treachery is here!
    Duch. Why, what is it, my lord?
    York. Give me my boots, I say. Saddle my horse.
                            [*Exit Servant.*]
Now, by mine honor, by my life, by my troth,
I will appeach the villain.   90
    Duch.   What is the matter?
    York. Peace, foolish woman.
    Duch. I will not peace. What is the matter,
      Aumerle?

95. **content:** calm.

100. **amazed:** dumbstruck.

101. **villain:** addressed to York's man.

106. **teeming date:** fertile period; childbearing time.

115. **He shall be none:** he shall not be of their number.

Aum. Good mother, be content. It is no more   95
Than my poor life must answer.
   Duch.   Thy life answer?
   York. Bring me my boots! I will unto the King.

         His Man enters with his boots.

   Duch. Strike him, Aumerle. Poor boy, thou art
     amazed.—   100
Hence, villain! Never more come in my sight.
   York. Give me my boots, I say!
                 [*Servant does so and exit.*]
   Duch. Why, York, what wilt thou do?
Wilt thou not hide the trespass of thine own?
Have we more sons? or are we like to have?   105
Is not my teeming date drunk up with time?
And wilt thou pluck my fair son from mine age
And rob me of a happy mother's name?
Is he not like thee? Is he not thine own?
   York. Thou fond mad woman,   110
Wilt thou conceal this dark conspiracy?
A dozen of them here have ta'en the sacrament,
And interchangeably set down their hands,
To kill the King at Oxford.
   Duch.   He shall be none;   115
We'll keep him here. Then what is that to him?
   York. Away, fond woman! Were he twenty times
My son, I would appeach him.
   Duch.   Hadst thou groaned for him
As I have done, thou wouldst be more pitiful.   120

V. iii. Aumerle by hard riding reaches the castle before his father and begs the King's pardon. His mother adds her entreaties to his own and the King consents to pardon Aumerle for his intended treason. He orders York to arrange for the capture of the other members of the plot.

∎∎∎∎∎∎∎∎∎∎∎∎∎∎∎∎∎∎∎∎∎∎∎∎∎

1. **unthrifty:** profligate.
7. **companions:** contempt is implicit in this synonym for "fellows."

But now I know thy mind. Thou dost suspect
That I have been disloyal to thy bed
And that he is a bastard, not thy son.
Sweet York, sweet husband, be not of that mind!
He is as like thee as a man may be,   125
Not like to me, or any of my kin,
And yet I love him.

    York.   Make way, unruly woman!   *Exit.*

    Duch. After, Aumerle! Mount thee upon his horse,
Spur post and get before him to the King,   130
And beg thy pardon ere he do accuse thee.
I'll not be long behind. Though I be old,
I doubt not but to ride as fast as York;
And never will I rise up from the ground
Till Bolingbroke have pardoned thee. Away, be gone! 135
                              Exeunt.

Scene III. [Windsor Castle.]

Enter King [Henry], Percy, and other Lords.

    King H. Can no man tell me of my unthrifty son?
'Tis full three months since I did see him last.
If any plague hang over us, 'tis he.
I would to God, my lords, he might be found.
Inquire at London, 'mongst the taverns there,   5
For there, they say, he daily doth frequent,
With unrestrained loose companions,

9. **watch:** night watchmen who patrolled the city streets.

10. **wanton and effeminate:** undisciplined and self-indulgent.

17. **stews:** brothels.

S.D. after 24. **amazed:** dumbstruck; panic-stricken.

31. **conference:** conversation.

Even such, they say, as stand in narrow lanes
And beat our watch and rob our passengers,
Which he, young wanton and effeminate boy,   10
Takes on the point of honor to support—
So dissolute a crew!

 Percy. My lord, some two days since I saw the
  Prince
And told him of those triumphs held at Oxford.   15

 King H. And what said the gallant?

 Percy. His answer was, he would unto the stews,
And from the common'st creature pluck a glove
And wear it as a favor, and with that
He would unhorse the lustiest challenger.   20

 King H. As dissolute as desperate! Yet through
  both
I see some sparks of better hope, which elder years
May happily bring forth. But who comes here?

   Enter Aumerle, amazed.

 Aum. Where is the King?   25

 King H. What means our cousin, that he stares and
  looks
So wildly?

 Aum. God save your Grace! I do beseech your
  Majesty   30
To have some conference with your Grace alone.

 King H. Withdraw yourselves and leave us here
  alone.   [*Exeunt Percy and Lords.*]
What is the matter with our cousin now?

46. **safe:** harmless.

49. **secure:** reckless; incautious.

51. **speak treason to thy face:** i.e., speak to you as I should not address my sovereign.

Henry IV.
From John Taylor, *All the Works* (1630).

Aum. Forever may my knees grow to the earth,   35
                                [*Kneels.*]
My tongue cleave to the roof within my mouth,
Unless a pardon ere I rise or speak.

King H. Intended, or committed, was this fault?
If on the first, how heinous e'er it be,
To win thy after-love I pardon thee.   40

Aum. Then give me leave that I may turn the key,
That no man enter till my tale be done.

King H. Have thy desire. [*Aumerle locks the door.*]
        The Duke of York knocks at the door and crieth.

York. (*Within*) My liege, beware! look to thyself!
Thou hast a traitor in thy presence there.   45

King H. Villain, I'll make thee safe.   [*Draws.*]

Aum. Stay thy revengeful hand; thou hast no cause
        to fear.

York. (*Within*) Open the door, secure, foolhardy
        king!   50
Shall I for love speak treason to thy face?
Open the door, or I will break it open!

                Enter York.

King H. What is the matter, uncle? Speak.
Recover breath; tell us how near is danger,
That we may arm us to encounter it.   55

York. Peruse this writing here, and thou shalt know
The treason that my haste forbids me show.

Aum. Remember, as thou readst, thy promise
        passed.

69. **sheer:** clear in the sense of being unsullied.
78. **lives:** i.e., will live again.
79. **my shamed life in his dishonor lies:** my life is shamed in his dishonor.

I do repent me. Read not my name there. 60
My heart is not confederate with my hand.
    York. It was, villain, ere thy hand did set it down.
I tore it from the traitor's bosom, king.
Fear, and not love, begets his penitence.
Forget to pity him, lest thy pity prove 65
A serpent that will sting thee to the heart.
    King H. O heinous, strong, and bold conspiracy!
O loyal father of a treacherous son!
Thou sheer, immaculate, and silver fountain,
From whence this stream through muddy passages 70
Hath held his current and defiled himself!
Thy overflow of good converts to bad,
And thy abundant goodness shall excuse
This deadly blot in thy digressing son.
    York. So shall my virtue be his vice's bawd, 75
And he shall spend mine honor with his shame,
As thriftless sons their scraping father's gold.
Mine honor lives when his dishonor dies,
Or my shamed life in his dishonor lies.
Thou killst me in his life; giving him breath, 80
The traitor lives, the true man's put to death.
    Duch. (*Within*) What ho, my liege! For God's sake
        let me in!
    King H. What shrill-voiced suppliant makes this
        eager cry? 85
    Duch. (*Within*) A woman, and thy aunt, great
        king. 'Tis I.
Speak with me, pity me, open the door!
A beggar begs that never begged before.

91. **"The Beggar and the King"**: an old song about King Cophetua and the beggarmaid.

97. **confound**: destroy.

99. **Love loving not itself, none other can:** that is, one who loves not his own flesh and blood can love no one else; hence his loyalty to you cannot be trusted.

King H. Our scene is alt'red from a serious thing,   90
And now changed to "The Beggar and the King."
My dangerous cousin, let your mother in.
I know she is come to pray for your foul sin.
    York. If thou do pardon, whosoever pray,
More sins for this forgiveness prosper may.   95
This fest'red joint cut off, the rest rest sound;
This let alone will all the rest confound.

Enter Duchess.

    Duch. O king, believe not this hardhearted man!
Love loving not itself, none other can.
    York. Thou frantic woman, what dost thou make   100
        here?
Shall thy old dugs once more a traitor rear?
    Duch. Sweet York, be patient. Hear me, gentle
        liege.   [*Kneels.*]
    King H. Rise up, good aunt.   105
    Duch.   Not yet, I thee beseech.
Forever will I walk upon my knees,
And never see day that the happy sees,
Till thou give joy, until thou bid me joy,
By pardoning Rutland, my transgressing boy.   110
    Aum. Unto my mother's prayers I bend my knee.
                        [*Kneels.*]
    York. Against them both my true joints bended be.
                        [*Kneels.*]
Ill mayst thou thrive if thou grant any grace!
    Duch. Pleads he in earnest? Look upon his face.

133. **meet:** suitable.
134. **Pardonne moi:** a polite refusal.
140. **speak:** express emotion.
143. **rehearse:** speak.

His eyes do drop no tears, his prayers are in jest; 115
His words come from his mouth, ours from our breast.
He prays but faintly and would be denied;
We pray with heart and soul and all beside:
His weary joints would gladly rise, I know;
Our knees shall kneel till to the ground they grow. 120
His prayers are full of false hypocrisy;
Ours of true zeal and deep integrity.
Our prayers do outpray his; then let them have
That mercy which true prayer ought to have.

   King H. Good aunt, stand up. 125
   Duch.   Nay, do not say "stand up."
Say "pardon" first, and afterwards "stand up."
An if I were thy nurse, thy tongue to teach,
"Pardon" should be the first word of thy speech.
I never longed to hear a word till now. 130
Say "pardon," king; let pity teach thee how.
The word is short, but not so short as sweet;
No word like "pardon" for kings' mouths so meet.

   York. Speak it in French, king. Say "Pardonne moi."
   Duch. Dost thou teach pardon pardon to destroy? 135
Ah, my sour husband, my hardhearted lord,
That sets the word itself against the word!
Speak "pardon" as 'tis current in our land;
The chopping French we do not understand.
Thine eye begins to speak, set thy tongue there; 140
Or in thy piteous heart plant thou thine ear,
That hearing how our plaints and prayers do pierce,
Pity may move thee "pardon" to rehearse.

   King H. Good aunt, stand up.

148. **vantage:** advantage.

152–53. **With all my heart/I pardon him:** re-arranged by Pope as verse; the Quartos and Folio read "I pardon him with al my heart."

155. **brother-in-law:** John Holland, Earl of Huntingdon, formerly holder of the title Duke of Exeter as a favorite of King Richard.

157. **consorted:** associated.

159. **order:** prepare; **powers:** armed forces.

Duch.   I do not sue to stand.   145
Pardon is all the suit I have in hand.
   King H. I pardon him as God shall pardon me.
   Duch. O happy vantage of a kneeling knee!
Yet am I sick for fear. Speak it again.
Twice saying "pardon" doth not pardon twain,   150
But makes one pardon strong.
   King H.   With all my heart
I pardon him.
   Duch.   A god on earth thou art.   [*Rises.*]
   King H. But for our trusty brother-in-law and the 155
       Abbot,
With all the rest of that consorted crew,
Destruction straight shall dog them at the heels.
Good uncle, help to order several powers,
To Oxford, or where'er these traitors are.   160
They shall not live within this world, I swear,
But I will have them, if I once know where.
Uncle, farewell; and, cousin, adieu.
Your mother well hath prayed, and prove you true.
   Duch. Come, my old son. I pray God make thee 165
       new.

                            Exeunt.

V. [iv.] Sir Pierce Exton has overheard the King express a wish for the death of Richard, whose life is a threat to himself. Exton decides to act as the King's friend and rid him of the dangerous Richard.

▓▓▓▓▓▓▓▓▓▓▓▓▓▓▓▓▓▓▓▓▓

3. **Have I no friend will rid me of this living fear:** Holinshed reports the King as saying, "Have I no faithful friend which will deliver me of him whose life will be my death and whose death will be the preservation of my life?"

8. **together:** consecutively; that is, having said it once, he immediately repeated it.

10. **wishtly:** wishedly; as if he wished me to act.

▓▓▓▓▓▓▓▓▓▓▓▓▓▓▓▓▓▓▓▓▓▓▓▓▓

V. [v.] Exton and his accomplices break in upon Richard at Pomfret, and though the deposed King fights valiantly he is finally cut down. Exton is at once repentant, but there is nothing to be done but to deliver the corpse to King Henry.

▓▓▓▓▓▓▓▓▓▓▓▓▓▓▓▓▓▓▓▓▓

1. **studying:** musing.

[Scene IV. Windsor Castle.]

Enter Sir Pierce Exton and Servant.

Exton. Didst thou not mark the King, what words
  he spake?
"Have I no friend will rid me of this living fear?"
Was it not so?
  Man.   These were his very words.   5
  Exton. "Have I no friend?" quoth he. He spake it
  twice
And urged it twice together, did he not?
  Man. He did.
  Exton. And speaking it, he wishtly looked on me,   10
As who should say, "I would thou wert the man
That would divorce this terror from my heart."
Meaning the king at Pomfret. Come, let's go.
I am the King's friend, and will rid his foe.

                         Exeunt.

Scene [V. Pomfret Castle.]

Enter Richard, alone.

Rich. I have been studying how I may compare
This prison where I live unto the world;
And, for because the world is populous,

8. **still-breeding:** ever-multiplying.

10. **humors:** dispositions.

12. **As:** such as.

13-4. **the word itself/Against the word:** i.e., one biblical passage against another.

15. **Come, little ones:** Matt. 19:14.

16. **It is as hard . . . :** Matt. 19:24.

21. **ragged:** rugged.

22. **pride:** prime. **Their** refers to the **thoughts** of l. 18.

main ism
content
why?

And here is not a creature but myself,
I cannot do it. Yet I'll hammer it out.
My brain I'll prove the female to my soul,   5
My soul the father; and these two beget
A generation of still-breeding thoughts;
And these same thoughts people this little world,
In humors like the people of this world,
For no thought is contented. The better sort,   10
As thoughts of things divine, are intermixed
With scruples, and do set the word itself
Against the word:
As thus, "Come, little ones," and then again,   15
"It is as hard to come as for a camel
To thread the postern of a small needle's eye."
Thoughts tending to ambition, they do plot
Unlikely wonders—how these vain weak nails
May tear a passage through the flinty ribs   20
Of this hard world, my ragged prison walls;
And, for they cannot, die in their own pride.
Thoughts tending to content flatter themselves
That they are not the first of fortune's slaves,
Nor shall not be the last; like silly beggars   25
Who, sitting in the stocks, refuge their shame,
That many have, and others must sit there.
And in this thought they find a kind of ease,
Bearing their own misfortunes on the back
Of such as have before endured the like.   30
Thus play I in one person many people,
And none contented. Sometimes am I king:
Then treasons make me wish myself a beggar,

41. **being nothing:** i.e., dying.

47. **check:** rebuke; correct.

48. **state and time:** kingly state and manner of life.

53. **watches:** sleepless moments.

54. **dial's point:** clock hand.

61. **Jack o' the clock:** the mechanical figure of a man that emerges to strike the hours or quarter hours in some large clocks.

63. **holp:** helped.

And so I am. Then crushing penury
Persuades me I was better when a king;   35
Then am I kinged again; and by-and-by
Think that I am unkinged by Bolingbroke,
And straight am nothing. But whate'er I be,
Nor I, nor any man that but man is,
With nothing shall be pleased till he be eased   40
With being nothing.   *The music plays.*
            Music do I hear?
Ha, ha! keep time. How sour sweet music is
When time is broke and no proportion kept!
So is it in the music of men's lives.   45
And here have I the daintiness of ear
To check time broke in a disordered string;
But, for the concord of my state and time,
Had not an ear to hear my true time broke.
I wasted time, and now doth time waste me;   50
For now hath time made me his numb'ring clock:
My thoughts are minutes; and with sighs they jar
Their watches on unto mine eyes, the outward watch,
Whereto my finger, like a dial's point,
Is pointing still, in cleansing them from tears.   55
Now, sir, the sound that tells what hour it is
Are clamorous groans, that strike upon my heart,
Which is the bell. So sighs and tears and groans
Show minutes, time, and hours. But my time
Runs posting on in Bolingbroke's proud joy,   60
While I stand fooling here, his Jack o' the clock.
This music mads me. Let it sound no more;
For though it have holp madmen to their wits,

67. **brooch:** ornament; perhaps a symbol of loyalty like a brooch worn as a badge on the hat.

68, 69, 70. **royal, noble, ten groats:** a pun on the coins of those names. A **royal** was worth ten shillings, a **noble** six shillings eightpence, and a **groat** fourpence. Richard means that having been deprived of his royalty he is now only the equal of the groom who salutes him and is thus not worth ten groats more.

72. **sad:** gloomy.

78. **earned:** obsolete form of yearned; grieved.

88. **clapping:** caressing.

In me it seems it will make wise men mad.
Yet blessing on his heart that gives it me!   65
For 'tis a sign of love, and love to Richard
Is a strange brooch in this all-hating world.

Enter a Groom of the stable.

Groom. Hail, royal prince!
Rich.   Thanks, noble peer.
The cheapest of us is ten groats too dear.   70
What art thou? and how comest thou hither,
Where no man never comes but that sad dog
That brings me food to make misfortune live?
Groom. I was a poor groom of thy stable, king,
When thou wert King; who, traveling towards York,   75
With much ado at length have gotten leave
To look upon my sometimes royal master's face.
O, how it earned my heart when I beheld,
In London streets, that coronation day,
When Bolingbroke rode on roan Barbary,   80
That horse that thou so often hast bestrid,
That horse that I so carefully have dressed!
Rich. Rode he on Barbary? Tell me, gentle friend,
How went he under him?
Groom. So proudly as if he disdained the ground.   85
Rich. So proud that Bolingbroke was on his back!
That jade hath eat bread from my royal hand;
This hand hath made him proud with clapping him.
Would he not stumble? would he not fall down
(Since pride must have a fall) and break the neck   90

96. **galled:** rubbed raw; **jauncing:** jouncing up and down as on a horse's back.

S.D. after 96. **meat:** food.

Of that proud man that did usurp his back?
Forgiveness, horse! Why do I rail on thee,
Since thou, created to be awed by man,
Wast born to bear? I was not made a horse;
And yet I bear a burden like an ass,   95
Spurred, galled, and tired by jauncing Bolingbroke.

Enter one [Keeper] to Richard with meat.

Keeper. Fellow, give place. Here is no longer stay.
Rich. If thou love me, 'tis time thou wert away.
Groom. What my tongue dares not, that my heart
     shall say.   *Exit.* 100
Keeper. My lord, will't please you to fall to?
Rich. Taste of it first, as thou art wont to do.
Keeper. My lord, I dare not. Sir Pierce of Exton,
Who lately came from the King, commands the con-
     trary.   105
Rich. The devil take Henry of Lancaster, and thee!
Patience is stale, and I am weary of it.
                           [Beats the Keeper.]
Keeper. Help, help, help!

The Murderers [Exton and Servants] rush in.

Rich. How now! What means death in this rude
     assault?   110
Villain, thy own hand yields thy death's instrument.
[Snatches a weapon from a Servant and kills him.]

V. [vi.] King Henry is told of the capture and execution of the traitors. Carlisle is brought in and is pardoned, though the King suggests that he live a retired life henceforth. When Exton brings the body of Richard, the King is anything but grateful; he refuses to reward Exton for the deed and vows a voyage to the Holy Land to atone for his own guilt in wishing for Richard's death.

||||||||||||||||||||||||||||||||||||||

3. **Ciceter:** Cirencester, spelled approximately as formerly pronounced; the modern pronunciation varies.

Go thou and fill another room in hell.
　　　[*Kills another.*] *Here Exton strikes him down.*
That hand shall burn in never-quenching fire
That staggers thus my person. Exton, thy fierce hand
Hath with the King's blood stained the King's own 115
　　land.
Mount, mount, my soul! thy seat is up on high;
Whilst my gross flesh sinks downward, here to die.
　　　　　　　　　　　　　　　　[*Dies.*]

　　Exton. As full of valor as of royal blood:
Both have I spilled. O, would the deed were good! 120
For now the devil, that told me I did well,
Says that this deed is chronicled in hell.
This dead king to the living king I'll bear.
Take hence the rest, and give them burial here.
　　　　　　　　　　　　　　　　Exeunt.

‖‖‖

Scene [VI. Windsor Castle.]

Flourish. Enter Bolingbroke [as King], the Duke of
　　York, with other Lords, and Attendants.

　　King. Kind uncle York, the latest news we hear
Is that the rebels have consumed with fire
Our town of Ciceter in Gloucestershire;
But whether they be ta'en or slain we hear not.

11. **At large discoursed:** related in full.
13. **worth:** merit; **worthy:** valuable.
16. **consorted:** associated.
22. **clog:** weight; burden.
24. **abide:** endure.

Enter Northumberland.

Welcome, my lord. What is the news?   5
    North. First, to thy sacred state wish I all hap-
        piness.
The next news is, I have to London sent
The heads of Oxford, Salisbury, Blunt, and Kent.
The manner of their taking may appear   10
At large discoursed in this paper here.
    King. We thank thee, gentle Percy, for thy pains,
And to thy worth will add right worthy gains.

Enter Lord Fitzwater.

    Fitz. My lord, I have from Oxford sent to London
The heads of Brocas and Sir Bennet Seely,   15
Two of the dangerous consorted traitors
That sought at Oxford thy dire overthrow.
    King. Thy pains, Fitzwater, shall not be forgot,
Right noble is thy merit, well I wot.

Enter Henry Percy and [the Bishop of] Carlisle.

    Percy. The grand conspirator, Abbot of Westmin-   20
        ster,
With clog of conscience and sour melancholy
Hath yielded up his body to the grave;
But here is Carlisle living, to abide
Thy kingly doom and sentence of his pride.   25

27-8. Choose out some secret place, some reverend room,/More than thou hast, and with it joy thy life: i.e., choose a secluded place, one more dedicated to piety than you have occupied hitherto, and there enjoy your life. The King pardons the Bishop but counsels him to live a life of religious seclusion in expiation of his past deeds.

35. Richard of Bordeaux: so called because Bordeaux was his birthplace.

38. slander: shame.

47. thorough: through.

52. sullen: gloomy; **incontinent:** without delay.

King. Carlisle, this is your doom:
Choose out some secret place, some reverend room,
More than thou hast, and with it joy thy life.
So, as thou livest in peace, die free from strife;
For though mine enemy thou hast ever been,   30
High sparks of honor in thee have I seen.

Enter Exton, with [Attendants bearing] a coffin.

Exton. Great king, within this coffin I present
Thy buried fear. Herein all breathless lies
The mightiest of thy greatest enemies,
Richard of Bordeaux, by me hither brought.   35
   King. Exton, I thank thee not; for thou hast
      wrought
A deed of slander with thy fatal hand
Upon my head and all this famous land.
   Exton. From your own mouth, my lord, did I this   40
      deed.
   King. They love not poison that do poison need,
Nor do I thee. Though I did wish him dead,
I hate the murderer, love him murdered.
The guilt of conscience take thou for thy labor,   45
But neither my good word nor princely favor.
With Cain go wander thorough shades of night,
And never show thy head by day nor light.
Lords, I protest my soul is full of woe
That blood should sprinkle me to make me grow.   50
Come, mourn with me for what I do lament,
And put on sullen black incontinent.

55. Grace: honor.

I'll make a voyage to the Holy Land
To wash this blood off from my guilty hand.
March sadly after. Grace my mournings here   55
In weeping after this untimely bier.

                                        Exeunt.

KEY TO

Famous Lines and Phrases

The purest treasure mortal times afford
Is spotless reputation.   *[Mowbray*—I. i. 186-87]

Truth hath a quiet breast.   *[Mowbray*—I. iii. 102]

My native English, now I must forgo;
And now my tongue's use is to me no more
Than an unstringed viol or a harp.   *[Mowbray*—I. iii. 170-72]

All places that the eye of heaven visits
Are to a wise man ports and happy havens.   *[Gaunt*—I. iii. 289-90]

Though banished, yet a trueborn Englishman.   *[Bolingbroke*—I. iii. 325]

This royal throne of kings, this scept'red isle,
This earth of majesty, this seat of Mars,
This other Eden, demiparadise . . .   *[Gaunt*—II. i. 44-72]

Eating the bitter bread of banishment.   *[Bolingbroke*—III. i. 21]

Not all the water in the rough rude sea
Can wash the balm off from an anointed king.   *[King*—III. ii. 55-66]

Of comfort no man speak! . . .
For God's sake let us sit upon the ground
And tell sad stories of the death of kings! . . .   *[King*—III. ii. 152-85]

I'll give my jewels for a set of beads, . . .
And my large kingdom for a little grave,
A little little grave, an obscure grave.   *[King*—III. iii. 156-63]

Down, down I come, glist'ring Phaeton,
Wanting the manage of unruly jades.   *[King*—III. iii. 187-88]

O that I were a mockery king of snow,
Standing before the sun of Bolingbroke,
To melt myself away in water drops!   *[King*—IV. i. 274-76]

Tell thou the lamentable tale of me.   *[King*—V. i. 47]